# DEATH AT THE DOCKS

Jim and Ginger Cozy Mysteries Book 4

Arthur Pearce

Copyright © 2024 Arthur Pearce

All rights reserved.

No part of this book may be reproduced, distributed, or transmitted in any form or by any means, including photocopying, recording, or other electronic or mechanical methods, without the prior written permission of the author, except in the case of brief quotations embodied in critical reviews and certain other noncommercial uses permitted by copyright law. For permission requests, please contact the author.

*"Death at the Docks"* is a work of fiction. Names, characters, businesses, places, events and incidents either are products of the author's imagination or are used fictitiously. Any resemblance to actual persons, living or dead, events, or locales is entirely coincidental.

ISBN: 979-8-3031-3979-4

# Contents

| | |
|---|---:|
| Chapter 1 | 1 |
| Chapter 2 | 15 |
| Chapter 3 | 29 |
| Chapter 4 | 41 |
| Chapter 5 | 53 |
| Chapter 6 | 65 |
| Chapter 7 | 79 |
| Chapter 8 | 89 |
| Chapter 9 | 103 |
| Chapter 10 | 115 |
| Chapter 11 | 125 |
| Chapter 12 | 139 |
| Chapter 13 | 151 |
| Chapter 14 | 165 |

| | |
|---|---|
| Chapter 15 | 177 |
| Chapter 16 | 191 |
| Chapter 17 | 203 |
| Chapter 18 | 215 |
| Chapter 19 | 225 |
| Chapter 20 | 239 |
| Jim and Ginger's Next Case | 251 |
| Bonus Content | 253 |
| Jim and Ginger's First Case | 255 |

# Chapter 1

The incessant buzzing of my new smartphone dragged me from my sleep. I fumbled for it on the nightstand, squinting at the screen's harsh glow. Three new notifications from "Celestial Alignments Daily" – Emma's latest contribution to my technological education. How she'd managed to sign me up for these alerts remained a mystery worthy of investigation.

"Your astrological forecast suggests an auspicious day for new beginnings," I muttered, reading the first message.

"Oh good, more cosmic spam," Ginger meowed from his perch on the windowsill. "Though I must say, the phone's vibrations make an excellent alarm clock. Much more effective than my usual method of knocking books off your shelves."

I swiped at the screen, attempting to dismiss the notifications. Instead, I somehow activated what appeared to be a meditation timer. Soft chimes filled the room.

"You know," Ginger observed, his tail swishing with amusement, "for someone who spent decades organizing library catalogs, you're remarkably inept at basic technology. Have you considered asking a kindergartener for lessons?"

"Very funny," I grumbled, finally managing to silence the phone. "I don't remember you being this chipper at eight in the morning."

"That's because someone promised to take me to the new bakery today." Ginger stretched languidly. "Don't tell me you've forgotten?"

I hadn't forgotten. How could I? Ginger had been dropping increasingly unsubtle hints all week about Sophie's bakery – the newly reopened establishment that had once belonged to her sister, Maggie. The same Maggie who'd tried to kill me in my living room just a few months ago.

"I don't know, Ginger," I hedged, swinging my legs out of bed. "Maybe we should give it a few more weeks. Let her get settled in."

Ginger fixed me with a penetrating stare. "Jim, it's been open for two weeks. The entire town has already sampled her croissants. Mrs. Abernathy claims they're even better than Maggie's, and you know how she hoards her opinions like Mr. Whiskers hoards bottle caps."

"That's not exactly a ringing endorsement, considering Maggie turned out to be a murderer," I pointed out, pulling on my slippers.

"True, but unless Sophie's poisoning people with pastries, I think we're safe. Besides," he added, his whiskers twitching, "I've conducted a thorough investigation through the kitchen window. Her technique with laminated dough is impeccable."

I raised an eyebrow. "You've been spying on the bakery?"

"I prefer to think of it as preliminary quality control." Ginger hopped down from the windowsill, padding after me as I made my way to the kitchen. "And I've noticed something interesting. She has an assistant – young woman, quiet type, makes the most extraordinary croissants I've ever seen through a window."

The smell of coffee gradually cleared my head as I considered Ginger's surveillance report. The morning light filtered through my kitchen window, catching dust motes in its pale beams.

"The girl has good hands," Ginger continued, watching me pour my coffee. "Gentle with the dough. Though she startles at the oddest things. Yesterday, a car backfired and she nearly dropped an entire tray of Danish pastries. Sophie caught them, mind you. Rather impressive reflexes for a baker."

I sipped my coffee, considering this detail. "Startles easily, you say?"

"Like a mouse at a cat convention," Ginger confirmed. "Though significantly better at pastry making. Speaking of which..." He fixed me with his most persuasive stare. "The morning rush should be dying down by now. Perfect time for a first visit, wouldn't you say?"

The smartphone chose that moment to buzz again. Another astrological alert, this one insisting that Venus's position favored culinary endeavors. I jabbed at the screen with perhaps more force than necessary.

"Fine," I conceded, setting down my coffee cup. "But if anyone tries to poison me with baked goods, I'm blaming you."

"Noted," Ginger purred. "Though I think your biggest danger will be death by technological incompetence. You do realize you just set that meditation timer for eight hours?"

***

The walk to the bakery took less than ten minutes, but each step seemed to carry the weight of memory. The last time I'd approached that door, it had been abandoned and locked, hiding Shawn's stolen whisky inside. Now, winter sunshine sparkled off new window displays filled with artfully arranged pastries and bread, while a freshly painted sign declared "Sophie's Sweet & Savory" in elegant script where Maggie's old sign had once hung.

The bell's chime sent a jolt of unwelcome familiarity through me as we entered the bakery. Despite the complete transformation of the interior – light woods, cream walls, and modern fixtures replacing Maggie's vintage aesthetic – this place still held dark memories. My hand instinctively touched my throat, remembering how her fingers had once tried to squeeze the life from me in my own living room.

"Oh, stop being so dramatic," Ginger muttered near my ankle. "Unless the croissants are armed, I think we're safe."

The display cases gleamed with fresh polish, showcasing an array of pastries that would have impressed even the most discerning food critic. Behind the counter, a young woman with red hair tied back in a neat braid worked with quiet concentration, arranging a tray of almond croissants. The door swung shut behind us, and though she glanced up briefly, her movements remained steady and precise.

"Welcome to Sophie's!"

I turned toward the voice and found myself face to face with Sophie Brown. The resemblance to Maggie was unmistakable – the same blonde hair, though Sophie wore hers shorter and less styled, the same brown eyes. But where Maggie's smile had been carefully crafted to charm, Sophie's held a frank openness that caught me off guard.

"Mr. Butterfield," she said, wiping her hands on her apron as she emerged from the kitchen. "I was hoping you'd visit eventually."

I hesitated, unsure how to respond. It was one thing to investigate Maggie when she'd been a suspect, but this – making small talk with her sister in a place that held such dark memories – felt surreal.

"Please," Sophie gestured to a small table by the window, away from the counter where a few early customers were examining the pastry selection. "Join me for coffee? I think we have some things to discuss, and I'd rather do it properly."

I found myself nodding, more from ingrained politeness than actual comfort. Ginger had already stationed himself near the display case, providing a running commentary only I could hear.

"The lamination on these croissants is exquisite," he observed. "Though I'm reserving judgment until I conduct a thorough taste test. For security purposes, of course."

Sophie returned with two cups of coffee and, to my surprise, a plate bearing one of the croissants Ginger had been admiring. She set it down near my chair, at perfect cat height.

"I noticed you brought your partner," she said, settling into the chair across from me. "Mrs. Abernathy mentioned he has quite the refined palate."

The coffee's aroma helped ground me in the present moment, its rich scent so different from the artificial vanilla Maggie had favored. Sophie waited while I took a sip, seemingly content with the momentary silence.

"I'll be direct," she said finally, her voice carrying none of Maggie's practiced charm. "I know this is awkward. Walking into this place can't be easy for you, given what happened."

"You seem well-informed," I managed, studying her over my coffee cup.

"Small towns," she smiled, but it held a touch of sadness. "And Maggie's letters, at least until they stopped coming. She told me her version of events, but I learned long ago to read between her lines."

In the kitchen, her assistant – Alice, the girl Ginger had mentioned during his surveillance – moved with quiet efficiency, her movements precise and controlled as she shaped loaves of bread. Unlike the nervous person Ginger had described from his window observations, she seemed almost serene in her work, though I noticed how she kept the kitchen door's clear line of sight to the front of the shop.

"Why here?" I asked, the question that had been nagging me since I'd heard about the bakery reopening. "Of all the places you could have started fresh, why choose the place where your sister..." I trailed off, unsure how to delicately phrase 'became a murderer.'

Sophie wrapped her hands around her coffee cup, considering the question. The morning light caught her profile, and for a moment the resemblance to Maggie was startling. But then she turned to face me directly, and the difference became clear – there was an openness to her expression that Maggie had never possessed.

"It wasn't an easy decision," she admitted. "When I wrote to Maggie in prison, suggesting I take over the bakery, I wasn't even sure she'd agree. We haven't been close for years. Even before everything that happened here."

She paused, watching Alice expertly transfer a batch of sourdough loaves to the cooling racks. The girl's movements were graceful, almost dance-like in their precision.

"But I kept thinking about what this place could mean to the town again. A good bakery is more than just a business – it's part of the community's fabric. Every morning coffee, every special occasion cake, every Friday treat that becomes a family tradition." She met my gaze steadily. "I couldn't let Maggie's actions be the final chapter in this story."

"Very poetic," Ginger commented, having finished his croissant with suspicious speed. "Though I have to say, her philosophy on community building is considerably more appealing than her sister's approach to customer relations."

The morning crowd had begun to thin, leaving just a few customers nursing their coffee in the corner. Through the kitchen doorway, I could see Alice beginning another batch of pastries. Her movements were unhurried but purposeful, and I noticed how she'd arranged her workspace to keep the front of the shop in her peripheral vision – not anxious exactly, but aware.

"Mrs. Abernathy recommended her," Sophie said, following my gaze to the kitchen. "Alice has a gift with the dough. Some people do, you know? They just understand it on an instinctive level."

"The dough doesn't lie," Sophie continued, absently tracing the rim of her coffee cup. "You can't force it, can't manipulate it into doing what you want. You have to work with it, understand it. Maggie never got that – she was always trying to control everything, make it perfect by force of will."

A timer chimed softly in the kitchen. Alice moved to check the ovens, her movements fluid and assured among her chosen domain. The aroma of fresh bread filled the space, rich and honest.

My phone buzzed again – another cosmic alert from Emma's astrology app. I fumbled with it, somehow managing to activate what sounded like wind chimes.

"Not quite mastered the new technology?" Sophie asked, amusement dancing in her eyes.

"The phone and I have reached an understanding," I said, finally silencing the device. "I pretend to know what I'm doing, and it pretends not to mock me."

"Modern problems," she agreed.

The front bell chimed as Mrs. Abernathy entered, Mr. Whiskers perched on her shoulder like some kind of furry gargoyle. The cat fixed Ginger with his usual imperious stare.

"Ah, the local food critic arrives," Ginger meowed dryly. "Complete with his mobile throne. Though I suppose we can't all conduct our bakery surveillance from ground level."

Mrs. Abernathy made her way to the counter, adjusting her glasses to peer critically at the day's offerings. "I see you've finally decided to give Sophie's a try, Mr. Butterfield," she called over. "About time. Her brioche would make those French bakers weep."

"High praise," I remarked to Sophie.

"More like a royal decree," she smiled. "Mrs. Abernathy's approval doesn't come easily. The first week we were open, she tested every single item we made. Took notes too."

"It was quite the inquisition," Sophie added, standing to refill our coffee cups. "Though after she declared our croissants 'almost as good as her grandmother's in Provence' – high praise from Mrs. Abernathy – the whole town seemed to relax. As if they'd been waiting for her verdict before deciding it was okay to come back."

I watched as Mrs. Abernathy conducted her morning inspection, Mr. Whiskers maintaining his dignified pose despite Ginger's theatrical eye-rolling from his spot near my chair.

"The town has good instincts," I said carefully. "They've learned to be cautious."

Sophie nodded, understanding my unspoken meaning. "They have. Which is why I'm trying to be just as transparent as possible. No secrets, no hidden agendas. Just good bread and honest work." She paused, then added more quietly, "I'm not asking anyone to forget what Maggie did. I just hope they'll give me a chance to create something new here."

From the kitchen came the gentle sounds of Alice working – the soft thump of dough being shaped, the whisper of flour being sifted. The morning light caught the dust motes dancing in the air, giving the scene an almost dreamlike quality.

"You know," Sophie said, breaking the comfortable silence that had settled between us, "growing up, Maggie was always performing. The perfect student, the charming friend, the reliable daughter. Even back then, everything had to be controlled, calculated, precise." She shook her head slightly. "But the bread knows when you're not being genuine. You can't fake your way through a proper sourdough."

I found myself nodding, understanding what she meant. The Sophie I saw before me was nothing like the carefully constructed persona Maggie had presented. Where Maggie had been all polished surfaces and practiced smiles, Sophie seemed comfortable in her own skin, flour-dusted apron and all.

"The true test of character," Ginger observed, eyeing the remaining pastries, "is not just in the quality of one's croissants, but in one's willingness to share them with distinguished feline critics. I'm pleased to note that our new baker seems to understand this fundamental truth."

I realized I'd stayed much longer than intended, the morning slipping away in the peaceful atmosphere of fresh bread and honest conversation. The early rush had faded, leaving just the quiet hum of the ovens and Mrs. Abernathy's detailed critique of the day's brioche.

Alice emerged from the kitchen carrying a tray of what looked like chocolate eclairs, each one glazed to perfection. She arranged them in the display case with careful precision. When a car horn blared outside, she paused briefly, her hands tightening on the tray for just a moment before continuing her work.

"You should try one," Sophie said, noticing my interest. "Alice has a way with choux pastry. She says the repetitive motion of piping the dough helps her think."

"Perhaps another time," I said, standing. "I should get going."

Sophie stood as well, brushing flour from her apron. "Thank you for coming, Mr. Butterfield. I know it wasn't easy."

"Jim," I corrected, surprising myself. "And thank you for... being direct about everything."

"Honesty is easier in the long run," she smiled. "Fewer ingredients to keep track of."

"Speaking of keeping track of things," Ginger meowed pointedly, "I believe we should establish a regular schedule for quality control visits. Purely for professional purposes, of course."

As if reading his thoughts, Sophie reached under the counter and wrapped one of the remaining croissants. "For later," she said, handing it to me with a knowing look at Ginger. "Consider it a peace offering. Not between us – I think we've managed that already – but between this place and its memories."

The morning sun had risen fully now, streaming through the front windows and catching the glass display cases, making them sparkle. The bakery smelled of butter and yeast and possibility – nothing like the artificial sweetness I remembered from Maggie's time.

"Feel free to come back anytime," Sophie called as we headed for the door. "Both of you," she added with a slight smirk. "Even if it's just to admire the croissants through the window."

Ginger managed to look both guilty and dignified. "I maintain that preliminary surveillance is a crucial part of any investigation."

As we stepped out into the late morning sunshine, I felt the weight of my memories of this place shift slightly. They didn't disappear – nothing could erase what had happened here – but they seemed less urgent somehow, overlaid with the fresh scent of honest bread and a quiet dignity of new beginnings.

My phone buzzed one more time – another cosmic alert from Emma's persistent astrology app. This time, though, I just smiled and slipped it back into my pocket. Sometimes, it seemed, the stars did know what they were talking about.

"I suppose," I said to Ginger as we walked home, "we could make this a regular stop."

"Purely for investigative purposes," he agreed smugly. "Though I notice you're not complaining about my window surveillance techniques anymore."

The morning had turned into one of those perfect winter days, the air crisp and full of promise. And for the first time since learning about Sophie taking over the bakery, I found myself looking forward to my next visit.

Even if it did come with a side of feline smugness and astrological notifications.

# Chapter 2

The January afternoon sun filtered weakly through our office windows, casting long shadows across the worn floorboards. The familiar scent of old books and coffee permeated the space, mingling with the faint salty breeze that somehow always found its way up from the harbor.

I sat at my desk, surrounded by the comfortable clutter of case files and mystery novels. The brass name plate – "The Oceanview Cove Investigators" – gleamed dully in the winter light, a Christmas gift from Sarah that still made me smile every time I saw it. Our case board stood nearly bare. A single yellow Post-it note about Mrs. Abernathy's missing garden gnome (Case Status: Solved – Raccoon Relocation Required) provided the only evidence of our recent investigative work.

Ginger had claimed his usual spot on his cat bed, his orange fur practically glowing in the afternoon light. His tail draped elegantly over the edge, twitching occasionally as he conducted what he insisted was "essential investigative napping."

"You know," he observed, cracking open one eye as I turned another page of my well-worn Raymond Chandler novel, "for a detective agency, we seem to be doing an awful lot of literary research lately. Though reading about murders is marginally better than solving them. Less running around in the cold, for one thing." He stretched languidly, showing an impressive array of teeth in a massive yawn. "And significantly fewer encounters with crazy booksellers."

The mention of Everett sent a familiar pang through my chest. He'd been sentenced to five years in the state penitentiary last week – three years for the thefts, plus two more for endangering public safety with that rigged Christmas tree. The stack of books he'd recommended still sat on my desk, their spines carrying the weight beyond mere paper and binding now.

My ancient flip phone – stubbornly surviving despite Emma's best efforts to upgrade me – sat silent beside a stack of invoices. The last real case we'd handled had been Everett's elaborate Christmas scheme, and since then, the most exciting thing to come across our desk had been the Great Garden Gnome Caper, as Ginger had dubbed it.

"Remember when we actually had mysteries to solve?" Ginger mused, rolling onto his back to catch a patch of sunlight. "Murderous bakers, treasure-hunting teenagers, holiday-themed crime sprees? Now we're reduced to tracking down lawn ornaments. Though I must say, watching Mrs. Abernathy lecture that raccoon about proper garden etiquette was almost worth the lack of dramatic chase scenes."

I smiled despite myself, remembering the elderly woman brandishing her umbrella at the unrepentant raccoon. "Sometimes quiet is good," I said, marking my place in the book. "After that Christmas case-"

"The Great Holiday Heist," Ginger interrupted, his whiskers twitching with amusement. "Featuring mechanical elves, deadly tinsel, and a surprisingly poetic bookseller. Though I still maintain that anyone wearing a green magician's hat should automatically be considered suspicious. It's like they're not even trying to hide their villainous tendencies."

The afternoon drifted by in comfortable silence, broken only by the occasional distant foghorn and the steady tick of the old clock on the wall. Through our windows, I could see the winter sun beginning its early retreat, painting the sky in muted shades of pink and gray. The streetlights flickered to life one by one, creating pools of warm light in the gathering dusk.

"Time for Shawn's," I announced finally, closing the book. The familiar weight of quiet routine settled around us like a comfortable blanket. "Unless you'd rather stay here and continue your investigative napping research?"

Ginger's ears perked up immediately. "And miss Shawn's latest attempts at creatively named cocktails? Never. Besides," he added, jumping down from his perch with feline grace, "someone needs to maintain quality control on his cream treats. It's a tough job, but some cat has to do it."

***

The walk to the Salty Breeze took us past Sophie's bakery, now closed for the day but still carrying the lingering scent of fresh bread and vanilla. Through the darkened windows, I could see Alice methodically wiping down counters. The lights were dimmed, but I noticed how she kept glancing up at any passing shadows, her shoulders tense despite the familiar routine.

The Salty Breeze's warm glow beckoned through the gathering dusk, its windows fogged slightly from the contrast between the heated interior and the bitter winter air. The worn wooden sign creaked gently in the evening breeze.

Inside, the familiar scents wrapped around us – polished wood, beer, the slight hint of salt that seemed embedded in the very walls, and whatever Shawn was cooking up for his daily special. The ancient jukebox in the corner was playing something soft and jazzy – Ella Fitzgerald, I thought, though the speaker's slight crackle made it hard to be sure.

The usual evening crowd had begun to filter in. Chuck nursed his regular beer at the end of the bar, a scatter of papers covered in calculations spread before him. Mrs. Abernathy held court at her favorite table, regaling her audience with the latest town gossip while Mr. Whiskers maintained his dignified pose on her shoulder.

"Jim!" Shawn called from behind the bar, already reaching for my usual glass. His checked shirt was rolled up to the elbows, showing forearms strong from years of carrying kegs and breaking up the occasional dispute. "Was beginning to think you'd forgotten about us, buried in all those books up there."

I settled onto my regular stool, its leather worn smooth by years of faithful service. Ginger claimed his customary spot beside me, arranging himself with the air of a king ascending his throne. The bar's surface bore the marks of countless stories – water rings, slight scratches, and what looked like fresh mathematical calculations scratched into the varnish.

"Someone's been doing their taxes at your bar," I noted, pointing to the numbers that meandered across the polished wood like a drunken spider's trail.

Shawn grimaced, setting down my drink – something amber and warming that he'd started making for me after the Christmas case. He claimed it helped with "detective-related stress." "That would be Chuck. Claims he thinks better with a beer in hand. Though judging by those calculations, I'm not sure the IRS would agree." He glanced over at Chuck's spread of papers. "Pretty sure seven times twelve isn't seventy-two, no matter how many pints you've had."

At a corner table, a group of fishermen were engaged in what appeared to be an increasingly heated discussion. Their voices carried across the bar in fragments, sharp with frustration and something deeper – fear, maybe, or anger. The words "quotas" and "regulations" cut through the general murmur of conversation.

"Liam's at it again," Shawn said quietly, nodding toward the table. His usual cheerful expression had turned serious, the lines around his eyes deepening. "Been stirring up trouble about commercial fishing practices. Says they're destroying the local marine ecosystem, driving away the fish populations." He picked up a glass, polishing it with more vigor than necessary. "Started some kind of environmental group. They've been following the boats out, documenting what they call 'harmful practices.'"

"The boat rental kid?" I asked, remembering the Christmas party fight. The image of Liam, face flushed with righteous anger, squaring off against a fisherman twice his size, was still vivid in my memory. "Thought he'd learned his lesson about picking fights with fishermen."

Shawn shook his head. "If anything, he's gotten more aggressive about it. Been posting videos online, naming specific boats. Started organizing protests at the docks." He set down the glass with perhaps more force than necessary. "It's not doing his business any favors, I can tell you that." He shrugged eloquently.

The argument at the corner table suddenly escalated, chairs scraping against the worn wooden floor as several men stood up. Liam's voice cut through the general noise, sharp with accusation and carrying an intensity I hadn't heard before.

"You can't keep destroying everything for profit!" His thin frame vibrated with barely contained emotion, hands clenched at his sides. The overhead lights caught the angles of his face, throwing shadows that made him look older, harder. "Someone has to stand up for the ecosystem before there's nothing left!"

Mike Sullivan – I recognized him from the Christmas party brawl – slammed his fist down on the table. Glasses rattled, beer sloshing over rims. His weathered face had turned the color of storm clouds. "We've been fishing these waters since before you were born, boy. Our fathers taught us, their fathers taught them. You don't get to come in here with your fancy internet research and tell us-"

"Everyone has a right to their opinion," I called out, my voice carrying across the bar. The room fell quiet, all eyes turning toward me. Even the jukebox seemed to pause, Ella's voice fading into silence. "But maybe we could express those opinions without property damage? Some of us are trying to enjoy our drinks."

Mike's face remained flushed, but something in his posture eased slightly. I'd helped him find his lost dog a couple of months ago – a gentle golden retriever with a habit of swimming after seagulls – and that seemed to carry some weight.

Liam, however, showed no signs of backing down. If anything, my intervention seemed to fuel his anger. "This isn't about opinions," he spat, his voice carrying an edge I'd never heard before. "This is about evidence. Facts. Data. You can't keep ignoring the damage you're doing." His eyes swept the room, challenging. "And anyone who stands by and lets it happen is just as guilty."

"Yes, because nothing says 'environmental activism' quite like picking fights in a bar," Ginger muttered, watching Liam with narrowed eyes. "Though I suppose shouting at fishermen is easier than actually implementing sustainable fishing practices."

Liam turned abruptly, nearly knocking over his chair. It teetered for a moment before crashing to the floor, the sound unnaturally loud in the tense silence. "This isn't over," he declared, his voice carrying that same strange intensity.

The door slammed behind him, setting the old brass bell jingling discordantly. Through the window, I watched his figure disappear into the gathering darkness, his movements sharp with barely contained energy.

The tension in the room gradually dissipated, conversations resuming at a more moderate volume. Mike and his companions settled back into their seats. Mrs. Abernathy had already pulled out her notepad, no doubt adding this latest drama to her extensive catalog of town happenings.

"That boy's going to get himself into real trouble," Shawn muttered, watching the door swing shut. He began mixing another drink, his movements automatic after years of practice. "Can't keep antagonizing everyone in town."

"He's changed since Christmas," I observed, thinking back to the party. Even during the fight then, there had been something almost playful about his defiance. This was different – darker, more driven.

"More intense," Shawn nodded, his expression troubled. "Started right after New Year's. It's like something snapped in him. Used to be a quiet kid, you know? Good with the boats, patient with tourists. Now he's all fire and fury about environmental causes." He glanced around before leaning closer, lowering his voice. "Between you and me, some of the fishermen are getting worried. Not about his protests – they've dealt with activists before. But there's something different about this. More personal."

"Sometimes people surprise you," I said, thinking of Everett and his elaborate schemes. "Not always in good ways."

"Indeed," Ginger commented, stretching lazily. "Though usually they have the decency to wait until after I've finished my cream treats before starting any dramatic confrontations."

The evening wore on, the bar's atmosphere settling back into its usual comfortable rhythm. The jukebox had moved on to Miles Davis, his muted trumpet weaving through the quiet conversations like smoke. The winter wind rattled the windows occasionally, making the warm interior feel even more inviting.

Shawn shared the latest town gossip as he worked – mostly harmless stuff about fence line disputes and noise complaints. But there was an undercurrent of tension in his voice when he mentioned the increasing conflicts at the docks.

"Robert's worried," he said, keeping his voice low as he wiped down the bar. The cloth moved in practiced circles over the worn wood. "Says the protest groups are getting more confrontational. Following boats out, documenting catch sizes, posting videos online. Making accusations." He glanced toward Mike's table. "It's making everyone nervous."

"Has anyone reported it to Miller?"

Shawn snorted, the sound carrying years of experience with our local law enforcement. "You know Miller. Unless there's actual violence, he's not interested. Says it's a civil matter." He shook his head, silver hair catching the bar's warm light.

Around nine, after watching Shawn create something he called a "Celestial Alignment" for Emma (who had stopped in briefly, trailing crystals and dire predictions about Mercury's retrograde), Ginger and I decided to head home. The night had turned bitter cold, our breath forming small clouds in the winter air. The streetlights cast pools of yellow light on the fresh dusting of snow, and somewhere in the distance, a foghorn mourned across the dark water.

As we passed the B&B – the former scene of both Maggie's crimes and Lily's treasure hunt starting point – I noticed a figure standing in the shadows near it. The building itself looked tired, its paint peeling slightly, windows mostly dark. The "Vacancy" sign flickered weakly, more habit than hope these days.

"Evening," the man said, stepping forward slightly. Something about his stance set off warning bells – too casual, too calculated. He was middle-aged, wearing an expensive wool coat that seemed out of place in our small town. The porch light caught the silver at his temples and glinted off what looked like designer glasses.

"It is," I agreed neutrally. A tourist, presumably, though the B&B's windows suggested otherwise.

"Interesting town you have here," he commented, his tone suggesting anything but casual interest. "Quite a history too, from what I hear. Murders, treasure hunts... makes for fascinating reading."

"Tourist brochures can be quite dramatic," I said carefully. Beside me, I felt Ginger tense slightly.

"Oh, I've been reading more than brochures," the man smiled, though it didn't reach his eyes. They remained cold, calculating behind the expensive frames. "Fascinating case, that Robinson girl. Made quite a splash in the regional papers. Bad for business though, I imagine." He gestured toward the B&B's empty windows. "Most tourists prefer their seaside holidays without quite so much excitement."

"I see our local hospitality industry has acquired its very own lurking shadow," Ginger observed dryly. "Though his technique needs work. If you're going to do the mysterious stranger routine, at least commit to it properly. The designer coat rather ruins the effect."

"If you'll excuse us," I said, moving to step past him. The temperature seemed to have dropped further, and not just from the winter night. "It's getting late."

He shifted slightly, not quite blocking our path but making his presence felt. "Of course. Just curious about local history. Always interesting to see how small towns handle their... darker moments." Something in his tone made my skin crawl – like he was conducting an interview only he knew about.

"You seem very interested in our town's affairs," I noted, studying him more carefully now. His stance, his careful positioning, the way his eyes never stopped assessing – this was no casual tourist.

"Professional interest," he replied smoothly. "I'm a journalist. Human interest stories, local color, that sort of thing." He produced a business card with a practiced motion, though I noticed he didn't actually offer it to me. The card caught the porch light, revealing glossy lettering from some regional paper I'd never heard of. "Always looking for interesting angles."

"I'm sure the tourist office would be happy to help," I said, finally stepping past him. His cologne – something expensive and trying too hard – lingered in the cold air. "Good night."

As we walked away, I could feel his eyes on us. The crunch of our footsteps in the fresh snow seemed unnaturally loud in the winter silence.

Once we were safely out of earshot, Ginger spoke: "Well, that was about as subtle as a foghorn in a library. Though I must say, for someone trying to play the mysterious stranger card, he rather overdid it with the prop department. The business card was a bit much. What's next, a cryptic note attached to a brick through our window?"

I glanced back, but the man had disappeared into the shadows of the B&B's porch. The building itself seemed to loom in the darkness, its windows like blind eyes staring out at the street. The Robinson case had indeed been bad for business – the story had spread through regional papers, painting our quiet town in sensational colors. Most tourists preferred their quaint coastal getaways without a side of attempted murder and dangerous treasure hunts.

We made it home without further mysterious encounters, though I noticed Ginger kept looking back occasionally, his ears swiveling to catch any unusual sounds. The night had grown colder, and I was glad to step into the warmth of our house.

Sleep came fitfully, my dreams filled with shadowy figures and half-heard conversations. The journalist's words mixed with memories of Everett's riddles and Maggie's smooth lies, creating a disturbing tapestry of deception and hidden motives.

*\*\*\**

The sharp ring of my phone cut through pre-dawn darkness, dragging me from uneasy dreams. Robert's name flashed on the screen, the blue light harsh in the darkness. Something in my chest tightened – Robert never called this early unless something was seriously wrong.

"Jim." His voice was rough, carrying an edge I'd never heard before. The sound of waves crashed in the background, along with voices I couldn't quite make out. "You need to come to the docks. Now."

I sat up, already reaching for my clothes. The bedside clock showed 5:47 AM, its red numbers seeming unnaturally bright. "What's happened?"

"It's Liam." A pause, filled with the sound of waves and what might have been sirens in the distance. Robert's breathing was uneven, like he'd been running. "He's dead. Found him tangled in my nets. I've called the police, but..." Another pause, heavier this time. "You need to see this."

"I'm on my way," I said, but Robert had already hung up.

# Chapter 3

Ginger, already alert and watching me from the windowsill, didn't need to be told twice. His night vision caught my expression perfectly. "Well," he said as I pulled on my clothes, "I suppose this means our quiet period is officially over."

The pre-dawn air bit at our faces as we hurried to my old Buick. A thin layer of frost had formed on the windshield, creating delicate patterns in the weak light from the street lamp. I started the engine, waiting impatiently as the defroster worked to clear the glass.

"Just once," Ginger muttered from the passenger seat, "I'd like to start a case at a reasonable hour. Preferably after a proper breakfast. Is it too much to ask for criminals to consider feline dining schedules?"

There was a tension in his voice that belied his sarcastic tone. We both knew that whatever waited for us at the docks would change everything. Again.

The harbor slowly materialized out of the pre-dawn gloom as we pulled into the parking lot. A heavy mist clung to the water, transforming familiar shapes into ghostly silhouettes. Emergency lights pulsed through the fog in an uneven rhythm, their red and blue reflections creating disorienting patterns on the dark water. The air carried the sharp bite of winter mixed with diesel fuel, salt, and something else – something metallic that made my stomach clench.

Fishing boats creaked at their moorings, their masts swaying slightly in the pre-dawn breeze. The sound of waves lapping against the hulls provided a constant undertone to the murmur of voices ahead. A small crowd had gathered near Robert's usual berth – mostly early-rising fishermen who'd arrived to check their boats, now standing in clusters, talking in low voices.

"Interesting how tragedy draws a crowd," Ginger observed quietly as we made our way along the slick dock. "Even at this ungodly hour. Though I notice our mysterious journalist friend isn't among the spectators. Yet."

"Give it time," I muttered, eyeing the growing cluster of onlookers. "News travels fast in small towns, especially the bad kind."

The wooden planks felt treacherous underfoot, slick with a combination of frost and sea spray. Each step required careful attention, the dock's surface reflecting the emergency lights like some bizarre dance floor.

Police tape fluttered weakly in the morning breeze, creating uneven yellow boundaries around Robert's boat. The Sea Witch looked different in the emergency lights – less the reliable fishing vessel I remembered from our island adventures and more like a prop in some maritime horror show. Each wave that slapped against her hull seemed to echo unnaturally in the pre-dawn stillness.

Sheriff Miller's bulky form was visible on deck, his winter coat making him look even more substantial than usual. His movements had the theatrical quality they always took on when he was trying to appear more competent than he felt. Two officers moved around the perimeter with the air of men who'd watched too many police procedurals on television.

Robert stood at the edge of the dock, his face ashen in the weak light. When he saw us approaching, something like relief flickered across his weathered features.

"Jim," he nodded, his voice rough. "Thanks for coming."

Before I could respond, Miller's voice carried across the water. "Butterfield! Should have known you'd show up. Clear accident case – kid was probably doing some of his environmental documentation, slipped on the ice. Tragic, but that's what happens when you mess around the docks at night."

"Yes, Miller's investigative prowess extends mainly to stating the obvious while ignoring actual evidence," Ginger commented dryly. "Though I suppose it's easier than doing real police work."

As we drew closer to the Sea Witch, I could see what had drawn everyone's attention. Liam's body was tangled in the nets hanging off the starboard side, moving gently with each wave. His dark jacket was soaked through, his face surprisingly peaceful despite the circumstances. One arm was caught in the netting at an odd angle, while the other floated free.

"Found him like this when I came to check my gear," Robert said quietly, coming to stand beside me. His hands were shaking slightly, and not just from the cold. "Called it in right away, but..." He trailed off, something flickering behind his eyes that I couldn't quite read.

The first real light of dawn had begun to creep across the harbor, revealing details that had been hidden in the darkness. There was a strange mark on the Sea Witch's hull, just above the waterline – a scrape that looked fresh, the paint scraped away to show bare wood underneath.

Miller clambered down from the boat with surprising agility for his size. "Open and shut case," he declared, pulling out his notebook with an air of finality. "We'll check the security cameras just to be thorough, but-"

"Cameras haven't worked in months," one of the officers interrupted, then immediately looked like he wished he hadn't spoken. "You were supposed to get them replaced after that vandalism case last spring, remember?"

Miller's face reddened slightly. "Yes, well, budget constraints..." He cleared his throat. "Anyway, clear accident. Probably trying to document something for that environmental crusade of his."

"Or suicide," the other officer suggested, not looking up from his notepad. "You heard how he was acting at the Salty Breeze last night. All that intensity about the environment. Maybe he just snapped."

"Amazing how quickly they jump to conclusions," Ginger observed, picking his way carefully around a coil of rope. "Though I notice nobody's asking the obvious question – like why someone so familiar with boats would be moving around the dock from this particular angle."

I studied the scene more carefully. Something about the position of Liam's body didn't quite match with either accident or suicide. The way he'd become entangled in the nets suggested he'd been moving through the water rather than simply falling in. And that mark on the hull...

The rising sun had begun to burn away some of the harbor's mist, revealing more of the scene. Scattered along the dock were small details that seemed out of place – scuff marks that didn't match the pattern of someone simply walking, a torn piece of fabric caught on a cleat that didn't quite match Liam's jacket, small things that together painted a picture different from Miller's simple accident theory.

The morning crowd at the docks had begun to grow. Word traveled fast in Oceanview Cove, and tragedy drew onlookers like moths to a flame. I could already see phones being raised to capture photos and video, their screens bright in the growing dawn light. In a moment of misguided solidarity, I pulled out my new smartphone, fumbling with the unfamiliar camera app Emma had installed.

"Really, Jim?" Ginger muttered as I accidentally opened what appeared to be a meditation timer instead. "Perhaps we should focus on actual investigating rather than contributing to the social media circus."

"Well," Miller announced, clearly happy to have an audience for his authority, "accident case. Probably fell in while doing his environmental documentation. Tragic, but that's what happens when you don't respect the water."

"A fall doesn't explain the mark on your hull, Robert," I said quietly, keeping my voice low enough that Miller couldn't hear. "Or the way the nets are tangled."

"Yes, but sometimes water does strange things, Jim. You know that from our trip to the island," Robert said.

The coroner's van had arrived, backing carefully down the narrow access road to the dock. Its white bulk looked almost obscene against the weathered fishing vessels, too clean and official for this world of salt and diesel. The medical examiner, Dr. Chen, emerged with her characteristic efficiency, her face showing no reaction to the growing crowd of onlookers.

"Sheriff," she called out after her initial examination. "There's something you should see."

Miller waved her off with his usual dismissiveness. "Already determined it was an accident, Doc. Just need you to make it official."

Dr. Chen's expression could have frozen seawater. "Perhaps you'd like to explain his bruised knuckles then? Or the-"

"Could've happened when he was trying to free himself from the nets," Miller interrupted quickly. "Let's not overcomplicate things."

"Heaven forbid we let actual evidence interfere with a conveniently simple explanation," Ginger commented, his tail twitching with irritation.

The morning light had strengthened enough now to show the harbor in its full detail. The Sea Witch's deck bore subtle signs of disturbance – rope coiled in unusual patterns, a broken gaff handle lying at an odd angle.

A sudden commotion near the crime scene drew everyone's attention. A young woman had arrived – I recognized her as Alice, the quiet assistant from Sophie's bakery. Her face was pale, her hands clutching her coat tightly around her. When she saw Liam's body being prepared for transport, she made a small, choked sound.

Miller had noticed her arrival too. "Miss," he called out, already moving toward her with his notebook ready. "This is a closed crime scene-"

"I thought you said it was an accident, Sheriff," I couldn't help pointing out.

Miller's face reddened. "Figure of speech. Now, if you'll excuse me..."

But Alice had already turned away, practically running back toward town. Her hasty departure drew curious murmurs from the gathered crowd.

"Curious how some people react to tragedy," Ginger observed.

Something was building here – a picture that went beyond Miller's simple accident theory. The way Liam's body was tangled in the nets, Alice's reaction, the physical evidence that Dr. Chen was still cataloging despite Miller's protests...

The morning had fully arrived now, turning the harbor's waters from black to steel gray. A trio of seagulls wheeled overhead, their harsh cries seeming to mock the solemnity below. The crowd had grown larger, their murmured conversations creating a constant undertone to the official activities.

"The bruising pattern suggests he was conscious when he entered the water," Dr. Chen was saying, her voice carrying the precise tone of someone used to being ignored by Miller. "And these abrasions on his hands-"

"Probably from trying to climb back onto the dock," Miller interrupted. "Case closed. Let's get him to the morgue and wrap this up."

"Remarkable," Ginger commented, watching Miller dismiss yet another piece of evidence. "I do believe our esteemed sheriff is going for some sort of record in willful ignorance. Though I suppose actually investigating would require him to miss his morning donut run."

The harbor's usual morning activities had begun to resume around us, creating an oddly normal backdrop to the scene. Fishing boats were heading out, their engines a steady throb across the water. The fish market was opening, its workers casting curious glances toward the police tape as they set up their displays.

"Hey," a gruff voice called out. "What's going on down there?"

Mike Sullivan, the fisherman who'd argued with Liam at the Salty Breeze, was making his way through the crowd. His face changed when he saw the coroner's van, the body being loaded. "Is that... is that Liam?"

"Afraid so," Miller replied, apparently glad for a new audience. "Accident case. Probably fell in while doing his environmental documentation."

Mike's weathered face showed genuine shock. "Jesus. We had words last night, but I never thought..." He shook his head. "Kid was passionate about his cause, I'll give him that. Even if he went about it all wrong."

"Quite the gathering of interested parties," Ginger observed dryly.

"Sheriff," Dr. Chen's voice cut through the growing murmur of conversation. "We really need to discuss these findings. The pattern of bruising, the abrasions-"

"File your report," Miller cut her off, already turning away. "Pretty clear what happened here. Kid was probably drunk after that scene at the bar, came down to do more of his environmental documentation, slipped on the ice."

He gestured vaguely at the dock's frost-covered surface. "Tragic accident, but that's what happens when you're not careful around water."

The crowd had begun to disperse as the body was finally removed. The morning sun had risen fully now, turning the harbor into a tableau of ordinary activity surrounding an extraordinary event. Fishermen prepared their boats with studied nonchalance, though their eyes kept straying to the police tape. The fish market's morning bustle seemed subdued, conversations muted.

Miller was wrapping up his official presence, already delegating the paperwork to the officers. "Clear accident case," he announced again, as if repetition would make it true. "Probably have the report finished by this afternoon."

Dr. Chen's expression suggested she had other ideas, but she kept her thoughts to herself as she packed up her equipment.

"You're quiet," Robert observed, still watching the water.

"Just wondering what really happened," I said. "Liam was passionate about his cause, but he knew these docks. Knew how to move around boats safely."

Robert nodded slowly. "Been thinking the same thing. Something doesn't add up here. Just can't put my finger on what."

"We'll figure it out," I said quietly.

The harbor had begun to return to its normal rhythm, though something had changed. The easy camaraderie of the docks felt strained now, conversations more guarded. Even the seagulls seemed subdued, their usual squabbling replaced by watchful silence.

As we walked back to the car, I could feel eyes on us – not just the obvious stares of the remaining onlookers, but others. More subtle observations from people who probably knew more than they were saying. In a small town like Oceanview Cove, secrets had a way of surfacing, like bodies caught in fishing nets.

"You're going to investigate," Robert said. It wasn't a question.

I turned back to look at him. The morning sun caught the silver in his beard, the lines around his eyes deeper than usual. "Would you rather I didn't?"

He was quiet for a long moment, looking out over the harbor he'd known his entire life. "No," he said finally. "Something's not right here. And Miller…" He shook his head. "Miller's already decided what he wants to believe."

"Indeed," Ginger commented as we got into the car. "Though I suspect the truth will turn out to be both simpler and more complicated than anyone expects. Humans do have a remarkable talent for that."

The morning sun painted the harbor in bright winter light, making the water sparkle despite the solemnity of the scene. But there was an undercurrent of unease in the air, questions that needed answers. Oceanview Cove had woken to a mystery, and as with all small towns, the truth would eventually surface.

"Home first," I said, starting the engine. "We need coffee, breakfast, and time to think."

"Finally, a sensible suggestion," Ginger approved. "Though I suspect our morning is about to get significantly more complicated. Small towns do love their mysteries."

As we drove away from the harbor, I caught one last glimpse in the rearview mirror – Robert still standing on his dock staring at the water, and Miller already heading toward his favorite donut shop, case closed in his mind if nowhere else.

But something told me this case wouldn't be as simple as Miller wanted to believe. People had a way of proving him wrong about these things – just like they'd done when he'd tried to pin Peter's murder on me, or when he'd written off Everett's Christmas schemes as a kleptomaniac spree. But that was fine by me. After all, finding the truth others missed was becoming something of a specialty for Ginger and me.

# Chapter 4

Weak January sunlight crept across my kitchen counter as I waited for the coffee maker to finish its morning routine. A cardinal perched on the back steps, its red feathers stark against the white backdrop, watching me through the window with beady-eyed interest. The thermometer outside read a brisk twenty-eight degrees, though the kitchen held onto its warmth.

The familiar aroma of dark roast helped ground me in the present moment, though my mind kept drifting back to Liam's body tangled in those nets, to Dr. Chen's careful observations, to the mark on the hull that told a different story than Miller's convenient accident theory.

"You're thinking too loud," Ginger observed from his perch on the windowsill. His orange fur practically glowed in the morning light, though his green eyes remained sharp and alert despite our pre-dawn wake-up call. "Though I suppose that's better than your usual attempts to operate that technological monstrosity Emma forced upon you."

As if on cue, my new smartphone emitted a series of cheerful chimes, indicating what appeared to be seventeen different notifications from various astrology apps Emma had installed. I fumbled with the device, somehow managing to activate what sounded like whale songs.

"Wonderful," Ginger commented dryly, watching my struggles. "Nothing complements morning coffee quite like electronic cetacean serenades. But it's an improvement over yesterday's meditation gongs."

Finally silencing the phone, I settled at my kitchen table with my coffee and notepad – the old-fashioned paper kind, not the electronic version Emma had tried to convince me to use. The morning silence settled around us, broken only by the distant cry of seagulls and the steady ticking of the clock above the stove.

"Let's go through this systematically," I said, pen poised above paper. "What do we know for certain?"

Ginger jumped down from his windowsill to join me at the table, his movements precise and deliberate. "Well, we know Liam was found in Robert's nets, showing signs of a struggle that our esteemed Sheriff Miller seems determined to ignore. The marks on his hands showed bruised knuckles and abrasions, according to Dr. Chen – though apparently, our local law enforcement considers evidence an optional part of investigation."

"And also that scrape on the Sea Witch's hull…" I added, making notes.

"Don't forget our skittish friend from the bakery," Ginger interjected, settling into a comfortable loaf position on the corner of my notes. "Alice's rather dramatic exit seemed rather significant for someone who supposedly had no connection to the deceased. Though I suppose finding dead environmental activists in fishing nets might upset anyone's morning routine."

I gently moved my notepad out from under my feline partner, earning an indignant tail twitch. "The question is, what was Liam doing near Robert's boat in the first place? His rental shack is on the other side of the harbor."

"Perhaps he was gathering more evidence for his environmental crusade," Ginger suggested, shifting to maintain his dignity after the notepad displacement. "Though one would think someone so passionate about marine life would know better than to investigate alone at night on a frozen dock."

The morning silence was suddenly shattered by what sounded remarkably like a foghorn blast emanating from my phone. I jumped, nearly knocking over my coffee cup. The screen displayed a name – Aaron Robinson – though how my phone had acquired his contact information remained a mystery. Probably another of Emma's helpful additions. We hadn't spoken since before Christmas, back when I still had my trusty flip phone. The last time we'd talked, he'd been telling me about Lily's improving grades and promising lack of treasure-hunting adventures.

"Emma's sense of humor continues to evolve in interesting ways," Ginger observed, watching me fumble with the device. "Using actual foghorn sounds as a ringtone in a coastal town seems a bit on the nose."

Finally managing to answer the call, I was greeted by Aaron's familiar warm voice. "Jim! Finally joined the modern age, I hear? Emma mentioned she'd helped you upgrade from that museum piece you called a phone."

"More like forced an upgrade," I admitted, smiling despite myself. "How were your holidays?"

"Good, quiet. Well, as quiet as they can be with teenage kids. Lily's science project only caused one minor explosion." He chuckled. "How about you? Emma mentioned something about an exciting Christmas case?"

"Let's just say I had an interesting holiday season involving mechanical elves and a rather dramatic New Year's countdown. Remind me to tell you the full story sometime." I paused. "How's Lily doing? Still staying out of abandoned tunnels?"

"Mostly focusing on regular teenage rebellion these days – though nothing compared to her treasure hunting adventure. She's actually doing really well in school." Aaron's voice softened with pride, then shifted to a more serious tone. "Listen, Jim... Emma called this morning. About what happened at the docks. Is it true about Liam?"

The shift in his voice told me he already knew the answer, but needed confirmation. "I'm afraid so. Found early this morning in Robert's fishing nets."

"God," Aaron breathed. The connection crackled slightly, carrying the sound of movement in the background. "We're visiting Lily's grandparents for the weekend – she overheard when Emma called this morning. She's pretty upset, actually. Would you mind… she'd like to talk to you. She keeps talking about how careful Liam was when she rented that boat from him."

Before I could respond, Aaron's voice became distant: "Hold on, sweetie, let me figure out how to… Emma said his new phone can do video calls… which button…"

"Oh no," I muttered, watching my screen suddenly fill with incomprehensible icons.

"Ah, the inevitable descent into technological chaos begins," Ginger commented, settling in to watch what promised to be an entertaining display of human versus machine. "I must say, your expression of pure panic when faced with a video call button is quite impressive."

The next few minutes involved a series of increasingly bizarre attempts to navigate my phone's features. Somehow, I managed to activate my camera, though it seemed determined to show only my ceiling fan. Aaron's voice floated through the speaker, offering helpful suggestions that only seemed to make things more complicated.

"Perhaps," Ginger suggested, watching me rotate the phone at increasingly improbable angles, "we should consider this abstract ceiling fan documentary your debut into independent filmmaking. The artistic choice to include your left nostril in such detail is rather avant-garde though."

Finally, after what felt like an eternity of technological warfare, Lily's face appeared on my screen. She looked older than during the treasure hunt case, her features more defined, though her eyes still held that same determined spark that had led her on her island adventure.

"Mr. Butterfield!" she exclaimed, then frowned. "We can only see the top of your head. You need to hold the phone up more... there! That's better."

Once the camera angles were sorted (more or less), I found myself looking at both Lily and Aaron, seated in what appeared to be a cozy living room. Family photos lined the walls behind them, and winter sunlight streamed through unseen windows.

"You finally joined the modern age," Lily smiled, though I could see worry lingering in her expression. "I can't believe about Liam. When Dad told me..."

She trailed off, and I could see her struggling to find the right words. Aaron placed a comforting hand on her shoulder.

"I just keep thinking about when I rented that boat from him," she continued finally. "During the treasure hunt? He was so careful about everything, you know? Made sure I knew all the safety procedures, showed me how to use it properly. Even though..." she glanced guiltily at her father, "even though I was obviously too young and offering way too much money. He could have just taken advantage, but he didn't."

"That doesn't sound like someone who'd take unnecessary risks on a dark dock," I mused, making another note. "Lily, did you happen to notice anything about his environmental work back then? Any signs or materials in his rental shack?"

"Not really," she shook her head. "I was pretty focused on the treasure hunt stuff. Though... now that you mention it, I remember seeing some posters on his wall. Something about protecting local marine life? I didn't pay much attention at the time."

"Did he mention any specific concerns?" I pressed gently. "About the fishing industry, maybe?"

"No, nothing like that. He was just really professional about the boat rental. It wasn't until I started following local news that I heard about his activism." She paused, biting her lip. "Dad showed me some articles about the protests at the dock. It seemed so different from the careful, safety-conscious person I met."

"Speaking of careful," Ginger observed from his spot on the table, "I notice our young friend has developed a more measured approach to investigation. A marked improvement from looking for abandoned tunnels and sailing into storms."

The smartphone chose that moment to emit a series of alarming beeps, and the screen suddenly split into bizarre geometric patterns.

"Oh dear," I muttered, fighting the urge to simply hang up and blame technical difficulties.

"Here, let me help," Lily offered, trying to guide me through the process of fixing whatever I'd done. "See that icon in the corner? No, the other corner. The one that looks like... actually, what happened to your screen?"

"I'm starting to think this phone has a mind of its own," I said, jabbing randomly at the display. "And not a particularly friendly one."

"That's debatable," Ginger commented, watching my struggles with evident amusement. "But your ability to accidentally activate features I'm fairly certain weren't included in the original programming is almost impressive."

Finally managing to restore the video to something resembling normal, I steered the conversation back to more relevant matters. "Aaron, has Emma mentioned anything else about Liam? Any other details?"

"Just that Miller's calling it an accident," Aaron replied, his expression skeptical. "But knowing Miller... well, let's just say we remember how helpful he was during Lily's case."

"That's one way to put it," Ginger muttered. "Though 'actively obstructive while maintaining peak donut consumption' might be more accurate."

The conversation wound down naturally, with promises to keep in touch and updates on Lily's schoolwork ("Much less treasure hunting this semester, I promise, Mr. Butterfield"). After several more technological adventures involving ending the video call – during which my phone somehow activated what sounded like a mariachi band – I finally managed to disconnect.

The kitchen settled back into morning quiet. A pair of cardinals flashed bright against the white as they visited my bird feeder, their movements precise and wary.

"Well," Ginger said, moving to reclaim his windowsill perch, "that was enlightening. And only moderately painful from a technological perspective. Though I do think we should work on your video call skills before you attempt any more virtual appearances. The detailed study of your ear hair was particularly riveting."

I ignored his commentary, focusing on my notes. "Liam was careful about safety procedures, even when offered extra money to bend the rules. Doesn't sound like someone who'd take unnecessary risks on an icy dock at night."

"And yet there he was," Ginger mused, watching the cardinals with predatory interest. "Tangled in Robert's nets with bruised knuckles and abrasions. Quite the mystery for our accident-adverse sheriff to ignore."

"We need to talk to Mike Sullivan," I decided, checking the time. The fisherman usually took his coffee break at the Rose's café near the docks around this hour – a creature of habit, like most of the local fleet. "That argument at the Salty Breeze wasn't their first confrontation."

"Ah yes, our friend with the impressive right hook and limited anger management skills," Ginger stretched languidly. "Though I suppose if someone were threatening my livelihood and organizing protests at my workplace, I might be somewhat irritable as well."

Standing, I gathered my notes and double-checked that my phone was actually in silent mode – no need for surprise mariachi bands during serious interviews.

"Ready to go do some investigating, partner?" I asked, reaching for my coat.

Ginger jumped down from his perch with feline grace. "I suppose someone has to keep you from accidentally broadcasting your nostrils to the entire town."

"At least my nostrils are more photogenic than Miller's accident theory," I replied as we headed out.

We decided to walk to the docks – the crisp morning air might help clear my thoughts. As we headed out into the bright winter morning, I couldn't shake the feeling that we were stepping into something more complicated than a simple accident. There were too many layers, too many questions without answers.

The town was fully awake now, going about its business with that peculiar mix of normalcy and underlying tension that follows tragedy in small communities. News travels fast in places like Oceanview Cove, but truth often moves more slowly, hiding in the shadows of assumption and convenience.

"Just remember," Ginger said as we walked toward the docks, the snow crunching under my feet (and somehow missing his paws entirely), "if anyone else suggests a video call, the answer is absolutely not. Some mysteries, like your relationship with modern technology, are better left unsolved."

"Says the cat who spent twenty minutes watching me struggle with the speaker volume a week ago," I muttered.

"Pure scientific observation," Ginger replied airily. "One must study the full extent of human technological incompetence to truly appreciate it. Though your ability to accidentally activate airplane mode while trying to adjust volume was particularly innovative."

The harbor stretched out before us, unchanged since our early morning visit except for the growing number of onlookers gathered near the police tape. Somewhere in this familiar scene lay answers about Liam's last night – we just had to find them. And preferably before Miller's determination to ignore evidence led to another case filed away under "convenient accidents."

We had work to do.

# Chapter 5

Rose's café sat nestled between weathered fishing shacks, its broad windows offering a panoramic view of the harbor. Steam rose from the ventilation system into the crisp winter air, carrying the mingled aromas that had become synonymous with comfort for the local fishing community – fresh coffee, sizzling bacon, fried fish, and most importantly, Rose's famous seafood chowder.

The morning sun glinted off patches of frost that still clung to the corners of the windows, creating prismatic patterns on the aged glass. Inside, warm air carried the lingering scents of breakfast mixed with the ever-present tang of salt that seemed embedded in the very walls. The ancient ceiling fans spun lazily overhead, their blades collecting decades of stories along with a fine patina of cooking oil and sea spray.

Mike Sullivan occupied his usual corner booth, the one with the best view of both the harbor and the door – an old fisherman's habit of keeping watch. His massive frame seemed almost too large for the worn vinyl seat, shoulders hunched forward as he cradled a mug of black coffee between hands that bore the marks of a lifetime at sea. The winter light emphasized every line and crease in his weathered face, making him look older than his fifty-something years. A fresh bandage wrapped around his right wrist caught my attention immediately, though he seemed determined to keep that hand mostly hidden beneath the table. I hadn't noticed the injury earlier at the docks, but then again, the crowd and chaos of the morning's discovery had made details like that easy to miss.

The bell above the door announced our arrival with a cheerful chime that felt discordant with the morning's somber events. The usual breakfast crowd had thinned to just a handful of regulars, all careful to keep their voices low as they nursed their coffee and studiously avoided discussing the discovery at the docks. The television mounted in the corner played a local morning show with the volume muted, creating an oddly silent backdrop to the scene.

"Morning, Jim," Rose called from behind the counter, her lined face crinkling into the warm smile that had welcomed generations of fishermen and locals. Her silver hair was pulled back in its usual neat bun, though a few strands had escaped to frame her face. She'd already survived the morning rush, but her white apron remained mysteriously spotless. "Your usual?"

She was already reaching for a bowl, knowing my weakness for her chowder. The ladle clinked against the large pot that had been simmering since dawn, releasing a fresh wave of aromatic steam into the air.

"Please," I nodded, sliding into the booth across from Mike. The vinyl seat squeaked slightly under my weight, the sound oddly loud in the quiet café. Ginger hopped up beside me with his usual feline grace, arranging himself with the dignity of a king ascending his throne.

"And a saucer of milk for your distinguished partner," Rose added, her eyes twinkling as she glanced at Ginger. "Fresh from this morning's delivery. Though after what happened at the docks, I almost added a splash of cream. Seems like a day for comfort food."

"Our culinary benefactor knows the proper way to treat an investigating feline," Ginger observed, watching Rose bustle away. His tail curved elegantly around his paws as he settled into a comfortable position.

Mike looked up from his coffee, bloodshot eyes suggesting a sleepless night. The bandage around his wrist drew my attention again – fresh gauze, professionally wrapped. "Figured you'd be by," he said gruffly, his voice carrying the hoarseness of someone who'd done too much shouting recently. "Miller's already been here, asking his useless questions between bites of donut. Seemed more interested in his breakfast than actually listening."

"I'm not Miller," I said simply, accepting the steaming bowl Rose placed in front of me. The chowder's rich aroma filled the air – fresh cream, local clams, potatoes, and that secret blend of herbs Rose had perfected over decades of serving the fishing community. A piece of her homemade sourdough bread, still warm from the oven, accompanied the bowl.

Mike snorted, his calloused fingers tightening around his coffee mug. "Clearly not. For one thing, you actually look at people when they talk. And your cat has better investigative skills than our entire police force." He paused, glancing at his bandaged hand before quickly tucking it back under the table. "Though I'm not sure that's saying much these days."

"High praise," Ginger commented dryly, delicately sampling his milk. "Though in fairness, a particularly observant barnacle could probably outperform Miller's detective work. At least barnacles stay firmly attached to their cases."

The café's ancient coffee machine hissed and sputtered, punctuating the morning quiet with its familiar rhythm. Through the windows, fishing boats moved across the harbor, their wakes creating white lines against the dark water.

"You want to know about last night," Mike said, his voice low enough that the other patrons would have to strain to hear. It wasn't a question. His fingers drummed an irregular pattern against his mug, betraying tension despite his attempt at a casual tone.

I sampled the chowder, letting the rich flavors settle on my tongue. Rose had outdone herself today – the perfect balance of seafood and cream, with just enough black pepper to warm the throat. "After that scene at the Salty Breeze, people will talk," I said carefully. "Especially now."

He grimaced, the expression deepening the lines around his mouth. A muscle twitched in his jaw. "Yeah, I figured. Look, I know how it looks. Big argument with the kid, then he turns up dead in the morning. But I was home all night after leaving the bar. Patricia – that's my wife – she picked me up. Didn't trust me to drive after that confrontation."

"What time did you leave?"

"Around ten. Maybe a bit after." He reached for his coffee, then seemed to think better of it, his hand returning to his lap. "Patricia wasn't happy about the argument. Said I needed to learn to ignore his provocations, keep my temper in check. She can be pretty fierce when she's disappointed."

"And after you got home?" I prompted, noting how Mike's gaze kept drifting to the window, tracking the movement of boats with the unconscious habit of someone used to watching the water.

He shrugged, the movement making his heavy fisherman's sweater stretch across broad shoulders. A few threads had started to unravel at the collar – the same sweater he'd worn during the argument at the Salty Breeze, I realized. "Watched some TV. One of those home renovation shows Patricia likes. Went to bed around eleven." His mouth twisted into a humorless smile. "Or tried to, anyway. She made me sleep on the couch as punishment for losing my temper at the bar."

"Notice how he keeps adjusting that bandage?" Ginger murmured, his keen eyes fixed on Mike's hands. "And the way his right sleeve is slightly damp at the cuff, like it's been recently washed. Rather thorough cleaning for someone who claims to have spent the night on his couch."

A particularly large fishing boat was passing through the harbor now, its diesel engine creating a low throb that vibrated through the café's windows.

"Tell me about the changes in Liam," I said, watching Mike's reaction carefully. "People mentioned he'd become more aggressive lately."

Mike's expression darkened, his weathered face settling into deeper lines. The morning light caught the gray at his temples, a reminder that he'd been working these waters since before Liam was born. "That's putting it mildly." He pushed his half-empty coffee cup aside, leaving a ring on the worn formica tabletop. "Kid used to be reasonable, you know? Even when he started his environmental campaigns, he'd talk to us, try to understand our side. Regular discussions right here in this café, actually. Used to join us for coffee, ask questions about sustainable practices."

Rose appeared with a fresh pot of coffee, topping off Mike's cup with practiced efficiency. Steam rose between them as she poured, carrying the rich aroma of her special dark roast blend. Her eyes flickered briefly to Mike's bandaged hand before she moved away, her rubber-soled shoes squeaking slightly on the linoleum floor.

"But something changed after New Year's," Mike continued, absently adding a packet of sugar to his refreshed coffee. His hands shook slightly as he stirred, making the spoon clink against the ceramic. "Started following boats out, filming everything. Not just general documentation anymore – he was targeting specific crews, posting accusations online. Got real confrontational about it."

The café's heat had begun to fog the windows slightly, creating a blurred filter through which the harbor activities seemed somehow distant, dreamlike. A seagull landed on the windowsill, peering in at us with beady eyes before taking flight again.

"Any idea what triggered the change?" I asked, breaking off a piece of sourdough to dip in my chowder. The bread was still warm, its crust crackling pleasantly as it absorbed the rich broth.

Mike hesitated, his fingers drumming against his mug. The bandage on his knuckles had started to spot with red in one corner. "Nothing specific. Though..." He glanced around the café, lowering his voice further. "There was this group from the city. Environmental activists, real hardcore types. They showed up at the docks about a month ago. After that, Liam was different. More radical."

"Like he was trying to impress them?" I prompted, noting how Mike's eyes kept drifting to the window, tracking the movements of boats and people with an almost obsessive attention.

"Maybe. Or maybe they just got in his head." Mike's jaw tightened, a muscle twitching beneath his salt-and-pepper beard. "Started talking about direct action, civil disobedience. Filming specific boats, specific crews. Next thing we know, he's organizing protests, disrupting loading operations to make some kind of point."

Ginger, who had finished his milk, was watching Mike with narrowed eyes. "Notice how he emphasizes 'specific' boats?" he meowed softly. "And that tension in his shoulders when he mentions filming? Our fishing friend seems particularly concerned about what might have been documented."

A group of seagulls had gathered on the dock outside, squabbling over something in their typically aggressive manner. Their harsh cries penetrated the café's windows, providing an oddly appropriate soundtrack to the conversation.

"The argument at the Salty Breeze," I said, steering the conversation back to last night. "What started it?"

Mike's face flushed slightly, the color creeping up from his neck to his weathered cheeks. His right hand clenched into a fist beneath the table, but the movement caused him to wince. "Kid was running his mouth, like usual. Showing people some video he'd taken of my boat, claiming we were exceeding quotas. Called us criminals, said we were destroying the ecosystem for profit." The words came out bitter, like coffee left too long on the burner.

"Been fishing these waters my whole life," Mike continued, his voice taking on a rougher edge. "My father taught me how to respect the ocean, how to fish sustainably. Three generations of Sullivans working these waters." He paused, staring into his coffee as if searching for something in its dark surface. "Then some college dropout with a camera phone comes along, telling me I'm destroying everything? Posting videos online, making accusations without understanding the first thing about commercial fishing regulations?"

The sunlight caught the collection of photographs on the café's wall behind Mike – decades of local fishing history preserved under glass. Weather-beaten faces smiled out from faded images, proud fishermen displaying their catches. I spotted a younger Mike in one of them, standing beside his father on what must have been his first boat.

"That must have been frustrating," I said neutrally, though I noticed how the tendons in Mike's neck stood out as he spoke, like mooring lines pulled too tight.

"Frustrating?" He barked out a harsh laugh that made several other customers glance our way. "Try infuriating. Do you know what those accusations do to a fisherman's reputation? How hard it is to sell your catch when some kid with a social media following labels you a marine ecosystem destroyer?" His bandaged hand emerged from under the table, fingers spread in agitation. "We've got regulations, quotas, oversight. Everything by the book. But one viral video claiming otherwise, and suddenly buyers are asking questions, demanding extra documentation."

The café had grown quieter, other customers pretending not to listen while catching every word. Rose busied herself wiping already clean counters, her movements deliberately slow. The wall clock ticked steadily above the grill, marking time in the tense atmosphere.

"Those videos he took," I said carefully, watching Mike's face. "Did he ever show any actual evidence of violations?"

The pause before his answer lasted a fraction too long. A bead of sweat traced its way down his temple despite the café's moderate temperature. "Course not," he said finally, but his voice had lost some of its certainty. "Kid didn't know what he was looking at half the time. Mistake normal fishing operations for something sinister because it fit his narrative."

"An interesting choice of words," Ginger observed, his tail twitching thoughtfully. "And quite the defensive tone for someone claiming complete innocence. Though I suppose being accused of maritime malfeasance might make anyone tetchy. Especially if there's truth behind the accusations."

Before I could press further, a commotion outside drew our attention. The seagulls scattered in alarm as a group of young people emerged from between the warehouses, their voices carrying through the café's windows. Several carried handmade signs with environmental slogans and Liam's name painted in bold letters. More were arriving by the minute, many wearing clothing adorned with marine conservation logos.

"Great," Mike muttered, his face darkening as he watched the gathering crowd. "Here we go. His eco friends, coming to stir up more trouble." His bandaged hand disappeared back under the table, but not before I noticed fresh spots of red seeping through the gauze.

The crowd was growing larger, their chants becoming more organized. "Justice for Liam!" echoed across the water, accompanied by the rustling of signs and banners. A tall man with dreadlocks and a megaphone seemed to be directing the group's movements, his voice carrying clearly even through the café's windows.

Mike pushed his coffee cup away with more force than necessary, making the liquid slosh dangerously close to the rim. His movements had become suddenly tense, like a fishing line pulled too tight. "I should go," he said, his voice rough. "Need to warn the others, make sure everyone stays calm."

"The others?" I asked, but he was already standing, his bulk casting a shadow across our table. The morning light caught something in his expression – not just anger, but something deeper. Fear, maybe.

"Other fishermen," he said shortly, pulling out his wallet. He tossed some bills on the table, his bandaged hand shaking slightly. "Look, Jim, I know you're trying to figure this out. But be careful. Some situations, there's no clean answers. No neat solutions like in your previous cases." His eyes met mine briefly, carrying a warning that went beyond words. "Sometimes the truth just makes everything worse."

# Chapter 6

The crowd outside had swelled to at least forty people now, their chants growing more insistent. Through the window, I could see them moving toward Liam's rental shack, where Officer Martinez stood guard beside the yellow tape. The young officer's hand kept straying to his radio, his posture radiating uncertainty.

The protesters carried a variety of signs – "Stop Ocean Destruction", "Justice for Liam", "Expose the Truth" – each one painted with the passionate intensity of true believers. Many wore sea-themed jewelry and clothing that marked them as part of the environmental movement. Their determination was palpable, even through the café's windows.

Mike was already heading for the door, his broad shoulders tense beneath his sweater. The morning light caught the fresh spots of red on his bandage as he pushed through the glass door, making the bell jingle discordantly. He moved with the purposeful stride of someone trying very hard to appear calm.

Rose appeared at our table, her lined face creased with worry as she watched the growing crowd through her windows. "Things are about to get complicated, aren't they, Jim?" she asked softly, gathering the empty dishes. "Like they did during the Maggie case?"

"More complicated," I admitted, leaving enough money to cover our bill plus a generous tip. "Though in a different way."

The man with the megaphone raised it to his lips, his voice booming across the harbor: "What is the police hiding? Why aren't they investigating the real criminals? Liam found evidence of illegal fishing practices – that's why they killed him!"

"Because actual investigation would require effort," Ginger muttered as we made our way to the door. "And we all know how Miller feels about exertion that doesn't involve pastry consumption."

The bitter winter air hit us as we stepped outside, carrying the mixed scents of salt water, diesel fuel, and impending confrontation. The protesters had formed a loose semicircle around Liam's rental shack, their signs waving like strange flags in the morning wind. Officer Martinez's hand had moved from his radio to hover near his belt, though his expression suggested uncertainty about whether to call for backup or try to handle the situation himself.

The crowd's energy had taken on a more aggressive edge. What had started as organized chanting was evolving into something rawer, more dangerous. The man with the megaphone – tall and lean, with dreadlocks pulled back in a neat bundle – moved with the practiced confidence of someone used to directing crowds.

"Your silence is complicity!" his amplified voice boomed across the harbor. "The evidence is in that shack! What are you trying to hide?"

Mike had stopped at the edge of the dock, his bandaged hand clenched at his side. Other fishermen were emerging from their boats, drawn by the commotion. The morning air crackled with tension, like the atmosphere before a storm. Even the seagulls had gone quiet, watching the scene unfold from their perches on nearby pilings.

"The truth about Liam is in there!" the protest leader continued, his voice carrying a passionate intensity that seemed to energize the crowd. "His documentation, his evidence – proof of what's really happening in these waters!"

The crowd pressed closer to the police tape, their movements becoming more aggressive. Officer Martinez's young face showed increasing strain as he keyed his radio, calling for backup in a voice that cracked slightly. The yellow tape stretched ominously as protesters pressed against it.

Through the gaps between people, I caught glimpses of Liam's rental shack. The small building looked somehow forlorn in the morning light, its weather-beaten walls holding whatever secrets had cost its owner his life. The window blinds were drawn, but something about their angle suggested they might have been disturbed recently.

"Look!" someone in the crowd shouted. "The door's been tampered with!"

The observation sent a ripple through the protesters. They surged forward as one, the police tape stretching to its limit. Officer Martinez's face had gone pale as he spread his arms, trying to hold back a tide of human determination with nothing but his presence and a badge.

"Stand back!" he ordered, but his voice lacked the authority to make it stick. "This is an active crime scene!"

"The only crime scene is what's happening in these waters!" the megaphone boomed. "What the police are trying to cover up! Liam knew the truth – that's why he had to be silenced!"

The yellow tape made a soft popping sound as it finally gave way.

"Stop!" Martinez's voice cracked with desperation. "Backup is on the way!"

But the crowd had tasted victory now. They moved forward like a wave, their combined purpose giving them momentum. The protest leader raised his megaphone again, triumph clear in his voice: "The truth can't be hidden forever! Justice for Liam!"

As the situation teetered on the edge of chaos, I noticed something odd. Through a gap in the crowd, I caught a glimpse of movement inside the rental shack – a shadow passing quickly behind the drawn blinds.

"We're not alone in our interest in Liam's sanctuary," Ginger murmured, his keen eyes fixed on the window.

The protest leader's voice boomed again through the megaphone: "What evidence did Liam find? What are they trying to hide?" Each question seemed to push the crowd forward another inch, like waves eroding a shoreline. Officer Martinez had backed up against the shack's door, one hand on his radio, the other raised in a futile attempt to maintain order.

More patrol cars were arriving now, their sirens cutting through the morning air, but they were struggling to navigate the narrow access road now crowded with protesters' vehicles. Even if they made it through, they'd have to find parking in the chaos that the usually orderly dock area had become.

The shadow moved again behind the rental shack's blinds, more deliberate this time. Whoever was in there was taking advantage of the distraction outside to search for something. But what had Liam hidden that was worth this risk?

"Fascinating how our mystery guest seems to know exactly where to look," Ginger observed, his tail twitching with nervous energy. "Almost as if they're familiar with the layout. Though I suppose breaking and entering during a protest shows a certain creative approach to criminal opportunity."

The crowd surged forward again, and Officer Martinez's radio went flying, skittering across the dock boards before falling into the gap between them. The young officer's face showed pure panic now as he pressed himself against the door, trying to physically prevent the inevitable.

"The truth about Liam!" the megaphone crackled. "The evidence he collected!"

Mike Sullivan had moved closer to the water's edge, his bandaged hand now shoved deep in his pocket. His eyes weren't on the crowd though – they were fixed on the rental shack's window, watching the same shadows we'd noticed.

A bottle crashed against the side of the shack, the sound making everyone jump. Glass scattered across the dock boards, reflecting the morning sun like diamonds. That seemed to be the final trigger – the crowd surged forward as one, overwhelming Officer Martinez's token resistance.

The first protesters reached the shack's door just as a new sound cut through the chaos – the deep, authoritative blast of the harbor master's horn. The noise was deafening at close range, making everyone instinctively cover their ears. In that moment of disruption, I saw a figure slip out the back window of the rental shack, moving with the quick efficiency of someone used to staying unnoticed.

They clutched something in their hand – papers, maybe – but before I could get a better look, they'd disappeared between the buildings that lined the dock.

The harbor master's horn sounded again, and this time Sheriff Miller's voice boomed through a proper police bullhorn: "This is a restricted area! Clear the docks immediately or face arrest!"

But I barely heard him. My attention was fixed on Mike Sullivan's expression as he watched the mysterious figure's escape. His face showed neither surprise nor confusion – only relief.

"Ginger," I said quietly, eyeing the gap between buildings where the figure had vanished, "can you track them? In this chaos, I'd never catch up."

My feline partner was already moving, his muscles tensed beneath his orange fur. "Consider it done," he meowed, his tail held low in stalking position.

He slipped into the crowd with the fluid grace only cats possess, weaving between legs and protest signs with practiced ease. His orange fur appeared and disappeared through the forest of bodies like a flame dancing through trees, steadily making his way toward the building gap where our quarry had vanished.

As Ginger disappeared from view, Sheriff Miller's voice continued to boom across the harbor, competing with protest chants that were gradually losing their fervor. The arrival of multiple patrol cars had begun to dampen the crowd's enthusiasm, their righteous anger giving way to more practical concerns about potential arrests. Officers were spreading out along the perimeter, their uniforms creating a blue line that slowly pressed the protesters back from the rental shack.

Through the thinning crowd, I watched Mike Sullivan's retreating back as he moved toward his boat. His posture was too rigid, his steps too measured – the walk of a man trying very hard to appear casual. The bandage on his wrist seemed brighter in the morning light, spots of fresh red soaking through the white gauze.

The man with dreadlocks lowered his megaphone, his intense brown eyes scanning the dispersing crowd. Up close, I could see he was younger than I'd initially thought, probably around Liam's age. A whale tail pendant hung from a leather cord around his neck, the silver worn smooth in places where worried fingers had touched it countless times. His dreadlocks were neat and well-maintained, tied back with what looked like recycled fishing line – a small detail that spoke volumes about his commitment to ocean conservation.

"You're the private investigator," he said, recognition flickering across his face. "The one who solved the Maggie case. Everyone in town still talks about it." He extended his free hand, the sleeve of his sustainable cotton jacket riding up to reveal a tattoo of waves circling his wrist. "Dylan Matthews. I worked with Liam on several conservation projects."

"Tell me about his evidence," I said, noting how several other protesters were drifting closer, drawn by our conversation. They formed a loose circle around us, their signs lowered but not discarded, like weapons at rest but ready.

Dylan's face darkened, his fingers unconsciously finding the whale pendant. The silver gleamed as he worried it, a habitual gesture that had left subtle impressions in the metal. "Liam called me two days ago." He glanced around before continuing, lowering his voice. "Said he had proof of serious violations."

A young woman with sea-green hair stepped forward, her hand resting protectively on Dylan's arm. The sleeve of her recycled plastic fleece was decorated with hand-embroidered dolphins. "He was determined, more determined than ever," she added softly.

"Tell me more about that," I prompted, watching their faces. Behind us, the officers had begun stringing new police tape, the yellow plastic whipping in the strengthening morning breeze.

"It was during a documentation run," Dylan explained, his jaw tightening. "We were tracking potential quota violations, using underwater cameras to monitor the catch sizes. Some of the local boats didn't appreciate our presence." He paused, choosing his words carefully. "But Liam didn't back down. Said he had a responsibility to protect these waters, even if it made him unpopular."

"He loved this harbor," the green-haired woman interjected, her voice catching slightly. "Knew every current, every tide pattern. The tourist boats were just his cover – his real passion was marine conservation."

Dylan nodded, his fingers still working the whale pendant. "Two days ago, he calls me out of the blue. Said he'd uncovered something major."

"Did he tell you what he'd found?"

"No, that's what was weird. Liam usually shared everything with our group. We were like family." Dylan's eyes drifted to the rental shack, now thoroughly surrounded by officers. "Said he had to be careful who he trusted. Whatever he found…" He trailed off, swallowing hard.

A commotion near the shack drew our attention. Officer Martinez, looking harried and overwhelmed, had accidentally knocked over a large metal trash bin while securing the perimeter. The contents spilled across the dock boards – coffee cups, paper bags, receipts, and other detritus of a rental business scattered in the wind.

As I watched the young officer scramble to contain the mess, something caught my eye. A piece of paper tumbled end over end, carried by the breeze until it fetched up against my leg. But it wasn't paper at all – it was a photograph, crumpled but intact.

I bent to retrieve it, the glossy paper smooth despite its crumpled state. As I carefully smoothed it out, the image stopped my breath for a moment. This wasn't the Liam from the protest videos or the angry environmentalist from the Salty Breeze. This Liam was different – younger somehow, his face relaxed in genuine happiness, his arm wrapped around a familiar figure that made my pulse quicken slightly.

Alice from Sophie's bakery stood beside him on what looked like the deck of a small boat. Her smile matched his, open and real, both of them caught in what appeared to be shared laughter. The harbor stretched behind them, painted in the golden hues of sunset. They looked... comfortable together. Connected in a way that went beyond casual acquaintance.

"Curious how quiet people can surprise you," I muttered, studying the details of the image. The mysterious figure who'd escaped through the window had been about Alice's height and build, had moved with the same kind of careful grace I'd observed in the bakery. But surely the quiet young woman who startled at loud noises couldn't be involved in something like this?

Dylan was trying to peer at the photograph, but Miller's officers had begun herding the remaining protesters away from the scene with more insistence. "Look," he said quickly, pressing a card into my hand, "that's my number. If you find anything about what really happened to Liam..." His voice caught slightly. "He believed in protecting these waters. Whatever he found, it was important enough to..." He couldn't finish the sentence.

The green-haired woman touched his arm gently, guiding him away as the officers pressed forward. The remaining protesters retreated in small groups, their chants had faded to murmured conversations, passionate energy dampened but not extinguished.

I studied the photograph again as the dock slowly cleared. The way they stood suggested the person taking the picture was someone they both trusted. Their body language spoke of shared secrets, private jokes, a comfort level that took time to develop. I carefully folded the photograph and tucked it into my pocket.

The mysterious figure, Mike's strange reaction, Alice's unexpected connection to Liam – pieces of a puzzle that didn't quite fit together yet. And somewhere in this web of relationships and secrets lay the truth about what had happened last night.

Once Ginger returned from his pursuit, we'd need to pay another visit to Sophie's bakery. Assuming, of course, that Alice was there and not our mysterious figure from the shack. Though the thought of that quiet young woman being involved in something like this seemed almost impossible. Then again, I'd learned the hard way that people in Oceanview Cove were rarely exactly what they seemed.

The rest of the harbor had begun returning to its normal rhythm, boats moving in and out, fishermen calling to each other across the water. But beneath this familiar pattern, something had changed. Questions hung in the air like the lingering morning mist.

What evidence had Liam found that was worth dying for? How did Alice fit into all of this?

More importantly, if Alice was indeed our mysterious figure, what had she taken from the rental shack? And what was she planning to do with it?

# Chapter 7

Police tape fluttered weakly in the strengthening breeze where the protest had been, yellow streamers marking boundaries that seemed increasingly meaningless. Most of the crowd had dispersed, leaving behind only scattered pamphlets that skittered across the wooden planks like pale ghosts of their earlier passion.

I leaned against a weathered piling, its surface rough against my back, watching Miller's officers gather the last pieces of evidence – if you could call crumpled protest signs and discarded coffee cups evidence. The harbor had begun to return to its usual rhythm, the steady thrum of boat engines mixing with calls between crew members and the endless cry of seagulls. The day felt surreal, as if the chaos of the protest had been some kind of shared hallucination.

A solitary fishing boat chugged past, its wake creating gentle ripples that made the remaining police tape dance. The fisherman raised a hand in greeting – most of the local fishermen knew me by now, though I noticed this gesture seemed more reserved than usual. News of Liam's death had changed things, creating invisible boundaries as solid as the yellow tape that still marked the crime scene.

I was considering my next move when a familiar orange shape emerged from between the buildings, looking decidedly less pristine than usual. Ginger's normally immaculate fur was ruffled in several places, his dignity apparently having taken a serious hit. Cobwebs clung to his whiskers like miniature battle scars, and a small but noticeable smudge of dirt marked his left ear, making him look like he'd been exploring places cats weren't meant to go.

"Good heavens," I said as he approached, noting his disheveled appearance and slightly indignant expression. "Are you alright? What happened?"

Ginger sat down with as much dignity as he could muster, immediately beginning to restore his appearance through careful grooming. "Well," he meowed, pausing to remove an especially offensive piece of cobweb from his whiskers, "it seems our mysterious friend wasn't the only one with territorial claims this morning. I had a rather... spirited discussion with the local feline enforcement officer."

"A cat fight?" I kept my voice low, aware of Officer Martinez still gathering evidence nearby. The young officer looked thoroughly demoralized after the protest debacle, mechanically picking up discarded signs while casting nervous glances at the growing crowd of onlookers gathering at the perimeter.

"Please," Ginger looked deeply offended, though the effect was somewhat diminished by the dirt smudge on his ear. "I prefer to think of it as a diplomatic incident involving conflicting jurisdictional claims. Though I must say, Mr. Mittens' approach to border security lacks subtlety."

"Mr. Mittens?" The name seemed absurdly incongruous with the gravity of our current situation.

"The self-proclaimed guardian of the warehouse district," Ginger explained, now working on smoothing his ruffled chest fur with meticulous attention to detail. "A rather imposing tabby with delusions of grandeur and questionable taste in names. Apparently, my pursuit of our mystery woman constituted an egregious violation of his sovereign territory."

A small group of locals had gathered near the crime scene tape, their hushed conversations carrying across the morning air in fragments. I lowered my voice further, conscious of how it might look – a man apparently having an intense conversation with his disheveled cat.

"So what happened?"

Ginger's tail twitched with remembered indignation. "There I was, maintaining a professional distance while tracking our suspect, when this walking dust mop appears out of nowhere, demanding to see my warehouse district traversal permit. Can you believe it? As if I need documentation to conduct an official investigation."

Despite the seriousness of the situation, I found myself fighting a smile. The sun caught Ginger's ruffled fur, making the cobwebs sparkle like tiny strands of silver. "And then?"

"Well, I attempted to explain the nature of my business, but Mr. Mittens proved remarkably resistant to rational discourse. Something about his territory, his rules, his power – you know how these self-appointed authority figures can be." He paused to address a particularly stubborn patch of dirt on his shoulder. "When diplomacy failed, he decided to express his disagreement in a more... physical manner."

"Hence the current state of your fur?"

"I may have been forced to take a somewhat unconventional route between some crates to avoid an international incident," he admitted, eyeing a particularly persistent cobweb with distaste. "Though in my defense, those cobwebs were very inconsiderately placed. And that dirt pile practically jumped out at me."

A gust of wind carried the sharp scent of brine and diesel fuel across the docks, making the police tape snap like small whips. Several of Miller's officers had gathered near Robert's boat, their postures suggesting they were mainly interested in appearing busy rather than actually investigating.

"But did you see who our mystery person was?" I pressed, steering him back to the more urgent matter.

Ginger's expression turned more serious, his grooming temporarily forgotten. "Yes, actually. Before my unexpected detour into feline foreign relations, I got quite close.

Definitely a woman, moving like someone who knows these docks well." He paused, whiskers twitching as he recalled the details. "She was carrying some kind of folder, probably full of papers or photographs. But here's the interesting part: when she was climbing over one of the low fences, her pant leg rode up. There was an anchor tattoo on her left ankle. Small, but well-done. Professional work."

I pulled out the crumpled photograph I'd found earlier, the one that had tumbled from the scattered contents of Liam's trash bin. "I have a theory about who it might be," I said, smoothing the photo carefully before holding it where Ginger could see.

The image seemed different now – Liam and Alice caught in that moment of shared joy on the boat deck, the harbor stretching behind them like a painted backdrop. Their easy familiarity spoke of a deeper connection than just baker and customer.

"The nervous girl from Sophie's bakery?" Ginger studied the image intently, his tail completely still – a sure sign he was fully focused. "The build matches, I suppose. And it would explain how our mystery woman knew her way around the docks." His whiskers twitched thoughtfully. "Though I must say, she looks considerably more relaxed in that photo than she does while making croissants."

"Think about it," I said, keeping my voice low as a pair of officers walked past. "Her nervousness at the bakery, the way she always keeps watch on the door – we assumed it was anxiety, but what if it was vigilance? And that startle response when loud noises happen – maybe it's not fear, but heightened awareness?"

A piece of police tape snapped free in the wind, whipping past us like a yellow serpent before catching on a nearby piling. The sound of boat engines and distant shouted orders drifted across the water as the harbor tried to return to its normal rhythm. The sun had strengthened, making the water sparkle almost painfully bright, like thousands of broken mirrors.

"We need to talk to Sophie," I decided, watching Miller direct his officers with his usual mix of bluster and vague gestures. "See if Alice showed up for work today."

\*\*\*

The walk to Sophie's bakery took us past the scene of Liam's discovery. The nets where they'd found him had been removed – evidence, presumably, though knowing Miller's department, they'd probably end up forgotten in some storage room.

The bakery appeared unchanged from our previous visit, its windows gleaming in the winter sunlight. Sophie had arranged the morning's offerings with artistic precision – rows of perfectly formed croissants, delicate fruit tarts that looked like jewels under the display lights, crusty baguettes arranged in a pattern that somehow managed to look both casual and precisely calculated.

The bell chimed softly as we entered, releasing a wave of warm air scented with butter and freshly baked bread. The contrast with the sharp harbor air was almost dizzying. The morning rush had passed, leaving only a couple of customers lingering over coffee at the small tables. Near the window, the journalist from the B&B sat studying his laptop intently, occasionally making notes in a leather-bound journal. He glanced up briefly as we entered, his expensive glasses catching the light, before returning to his work with studied nonchalance.

But there was no sign of Alice behind the counter or in the kitchen.

Sophie looked up from where she was arranging a fresh batch of croissants, her movements precise and efficient. She'd tied her blonde hair back with a blue bandana that matched her apron. A smudge of flour on her cheek somehow made her look more approachable, more real than Maggie ever had.

"Jim," she greeted me, her smile genuine but touched with sadness. "Horrible business down at the docks. News travels fast in small towns." She glanced around her quiet bakery. "Though not fast enough to keep people from wanting their morning pastries, thank goodness. Can I get you anything?"

"Just coffee," I said. "Already had late breakfast at Rose's."

"Ah, the famous chowder," Sophie nodded, moving to the coffee station. Her movements were smooth and practiced, but I noticed a slight tension in her shoulders. "I've tried to recreate it, you know. Can't quite get it right. Rose guards that recipe like it's a state secret."

The espresso machine hissed and gurgled as Sophie worked, its mechanical sounds mixing with the rapid clicks of the journalist's laptop keyboard. The rich aroma of fresh coffee filled the air, mingling with the lingering scents of baked goods. Everything felt deceptively normal, as if the chaos at the docks had happened in another world entirely.

"I heard there was some excitement at the docks this morning," Sophie said carefully, steaming milk for my latte. "Besides the... obvious. Protests, I think someone said?"

"Word travels fast," I observed, watching her face.

"Small towns," she shrugged. "Though I have to admit, I've been a bit distracted this morning. Short-handed today."

"I noticed Alice isn't here," I said, keeping my tone casual.

Sophie's hands paused briefly in their work, a barely noticeable hesitation before she continued crafting the latte. "No, she asked for the day off. Under the circum stances..." She trailed off, focusing intently on creating a perfect leaf pattern in the foam.

"The circumstances?"

She set the finished coffee in front of me. The leaf pattern was flawless, I noticed – each line precise and delicate.

Sophie was quiet for a moment, apparently debating how much to say.

"It hit her hard," she said finally, wiping her hands on her apron. "The news about Liam. I mean, of course it would. They were together."

The coffee cup paused halfway to my lips, the perfectly crafted leaf pattern blurring as my hand went still. "Together?"

Sophie's expression softened with something like sympathy. "You didn't know? Alice and Liam were dating. Had been for over a year, I think."

The photograph in my pocket suddenly felt as heavy as a stone.

# Chapter 8

Sophie's revelation about Alice and Liam's relationship hung in the air between us, adding another layer to an already complex puzzle. The sunlight filtering through the bakery windows caught the steam rising from my coffee, the perfect leaf pattern in the foam slowly dissolving into formless swirls.

"That explains her reaction at the crime scene," I mused, more to myself than Sophie, remembering Alice's pale face and hasty departure. "Though it raises more questions than it answers." The girl I'd observed in the bakery, quietly crafting perfect croissants with nervous energy, seemed an unlikely suspect for murder. But then again, so had Maggie, with her carefully crafted persona of small-town baker.

"Questions?" Sophie's hands kept moving as she reorganized the display case, but I noticed how her movements had become more deliberate, almost cautious. Her blue bandana had slipped slightly, letting a strand of blonde hair fall across her face. She tucked it back with a flour-dusted hand, leaving a faint white smudge on her cheek.

"I had no idea they were dating," I said carefully, watching her face.

Sophie's laugh held little humor, the sound echoing slightly in the near-empty space. "I barely knew myself, to be honest. Alice isn't exactly chatty about her personal life. Most days I was lucky to get more than 'good morning' and 'goodbye' from her." She paused, adjusting a row of croissants. "Though that changed about a week ago."

"Oh?" I took a sip of my coffee, noting how the journalist by the window had shifted slightly in his chair, his typing becoming noticeably slower. His leather-bound notebook lay open beside his laptop, its pages covered in what looked like hastily scribbled observations. He tilted his head, clearly trying to catch our conversation while pretending to be absorbed in his work.

"She came in different that morning," Sophie continued, her voice lowered as she pretended to adjust pastries that were already perfectly aligned. "Not her usual quiet self. More... scattered. More nervous. Kept dropping things, jumping at small noises more than usual. Broke two mixing bowls in one morning – I'd never seen her break anything before." She glanced around the bakery before adding, "When I finally got her to talk, she mentioned some trouble with her boyfriend. Didn't give details, but something was clearly wrong."

The coffee suddenly tasted bitter on my tongue.

"Wrong how?"

Sophie's hands stilled on the display case, her reflection fractured across the curved glass. The espresso machine dripped steadily in the background, each drop marking time like a metronome. "I don't know exactly. She wouldn't say. But..." She bit her lip, clearly wrestling with whether to continue. "There was something in her voice, the way she carried herself. Made me wonder if maybe Liam had..." She trailed off, unable or unwilling to finish the thought.

"If he'd hurt her?" I prompted gently.

The espresso machine chose that moment to release a burst of steam, making us both jump. The journalist's typing had stopped entirely now, though he maintained a studying pretense of focusing on his screen. His coffee sat untouched, a ring of condensation forming around the base of the cup.

"I shouldn't have said anything," Sophie backtracked, wiping her hands nervously on her apron, leaving floury streaks across the blue fabric. "It was probably nothing. Just me reading too much into things. Alice is naturally quiet, you know? Sometimes quiet people just have quiet days."

The photograph felt heavy in my pocket as I considered the implications. The happy couple on the boat seemed at odds with Sophie's hints of trouble. "Sophie," I said carefully, "given what happened to Liam... is it possible that Alice-"

"No!" The force of her denial made a customer at the corner table look up from his newspaper, the pages rustling loudly in the sudden silence. Sophie lowered her voice, leaning closer over the counter. The scent of yeast clung to her clothes. "No, absolutely not. Alice wouldn't hurt anyone. She's sweet, gentle. Sometimes I worry she's too gentle for this world. Yesterday she spent an hour scattering bread crumbs for the cardinal family that visits our back steps, making sure each bird got its fair share."

"Like Maggie seemed sweet?" The words left my mouth before I could stop them.

Sophie's face hardened slightly, reminding me suddenly of her sister. The family resemblance, usually subtle, became more pronounced. "That's not fair, Jim. You can't suspect everyone just because a few people turned out to be different than they appeared. You're starting to sound like Miller, seeing killers behind every counter."

"Can't I?" I thought of Maggie's perfectly crafted persona, of Everett's carefully maintained facade. The cooling coffee between us seemed to represent the growing distance in our conversation. "People in this town have a habit of surprising me, Sophie. Not always in good ways."

"Ain't that the truth," Ginger commented, stretching lazily. "Our track record with seemingly innocent townspeople is rather concerning. Perhaps we should consider relocating to somewhere with a more straightforward criminal element. I hear big cities are lovely this time of year. At least their murderers have the decency to act suspicious from the start."

Sophie was quiet for a moment, absently straightening items that were already perfectly arranged. Her movements had the automatic quality of someone whose hands needed occupation while their mind was elsewhere. The sunlight caught the flour dust in the air, making it look like shimmer around her. Finally, she said, "You want to talk to her, don't you?"

"I need to, yes. Where does she live?"

She hesitated, then reached for the order pad by the register. The blue leather cover was worn smooth in places from countless orders taken. "I'll write down her address. But Jim?" She looked up, her expression serious, a smudge of flour still marking her cheek like war paint. "Be gentle. Whatever happened between her and Liam, she's hurting right now."

"Assuming she didn't cause that hurt herself," I couldn't help adding.

Sophie's pen paused on the paper, the scratching sound suddenly silent. A delivery truck rumbled past outside, making the pastry displays vibrate slightly. "You really think she could have killed him?"

"I think I can't rule out any possibilities yet. Not until I have more answers." The journalist had given up all pretense of working now, his head tilted more toward our conversation.

She finished writing and tore off the page, but didn't immediately hand it over. The paper trembled slightly in her grip. "She might not want to talk right now."

"That's her choice. But I still need to try."

Sophie nodded slowly and passed me the paper. Her handwriting was neat and precise, nothing like Maggie's flowing script. "Just... remember that not everyone who seems suspicious is guilty. Sometimes quiet people are just quiet."

"And sometimes they're hiding something," I mused, tucking the address into my pocket alongside the photograph. The two pieces of paper seemed to weigh more than they should.

\*\*\*

I left enough money on the counter to cover the coffee, thanked Sophie and headed for the door, Ginger falling into step beside me.

"You know," he said as we stepped outside, "it occurs to me that this investigation would be significantly easier if humans simply followed the feline approach to relationship disputes. A few strategic hisses, perhaps a well-timed swat, and everyone moves on with their lives."

"Right, your solution to Mr. Whiskers stealing your sunning spot was so diplomatic," I muttered, remembering the yowling match that had kept half the neighborhood awake last week.

The street had grown busier, locals going about their morning routines with the studied nonchalance of people trying not to appear too interested in recent events. A group of fishermen passed by, their voices hushed as they discussed something that fell silent as soon as they noticed me.

The address Sophie had given me was on Pinewood Street. I assumed it was in that quiet residential area away from the harbor's constant activity, but I hadn't explored much of that part of town. "Do you know where this street is?" I asked Ginger, showing him the paper.

He gave me a look that managed to convey several levels of disdain, his whiskers twitching with barely contained amusement. "I'm a cat, Jim. I navigate by landmarks, scents, and an innate sense of superiority. Street names are a human construct that I choose to ignore."

"Helpful as always," I muttered, pulling out my new smartphone. The screen caught the sunlight, making it nearly impossible to read. "I suppose it's time to figure out how this GPS thing works."

"Oh, wonderful," Ginger settled in to watch what promised to be an entertaining performance, finding a comfortable spot on a nearby bench. His tail curled around his paws with elegant precision. "I do so enjoy our technological adventures. Should I alert the emergency services now, or wait until we're thoroughly lost?"

The phone's screen seemed unnecessarily bright even after I managed to shade it with my hand. The Maps app presented a bewildering array of options, icons, and features that seemed designed specifically to confuse anyone over sixty. The interface appeared to have been created by someone who assumed users had grown up with technology in their cribs.

"Type your destination," the phone prompted cheerfully, its artificial cheerfulness somehow making the whole process more annoying. I did as instructed, carefully pecking out each letter with one finger.

"Recalculating," the phone announced after a moment, its feminine voice sounding suspiciously like Emma's meditation app. "GPS signal not found."

"What do you mean, not found?" I demanded, turning the phone different angles as if that might help. A passing dog-walker gave me an odd look as I held the device toward the sky. "It's right there on the screen!"

"Is there perhaps a small detail you've forgotten?" Ginger asked, watching me wave the phone at the sky like some kind of technological dowsing rod. "Something about activating the actual navigation function?"

I lowered the phone, frowning at the screen. "What do you mean?"

"The GPS, old man. That little satellite icon you've been studiously ignoring for the past five minutes."

"I knew that," I muttered, though of course I hadn't.

After several more minutes of fumbling, during which I somehow managed to change the phone's language to Spanish and back, I finally located the GPS settings. The satellite icon, once pointed out, seemed obvious – though I'd never admit that to my smirking audience.

"Turn right in 200 feet," the phone instructed in what definitely sounded like Emma's meditation app voice. I had a sneaking suspicion she'd somehow managed to personalize my navigation system during one of her "helpful" technology sessions.

I turned right, following the blue line on the screen.

"Recalculating," the phone announced cheerfully. "Make a U-turn when possible."

"But you just told me to turn right!"

"I believe," Ginger observed, watching me spin in a complete circle while holding the phone at increasingly improbable angles, "that you've managed to confuse both the GPS and yourself. Quite an achievement, really. Though I must say, watching you argue with an inanimate object does add a certain theatrical element to our investigation."

"At least I don't get into philosophical debates with the bathroom mirror," I murmured, remembering his morning grooming sessions that often involved lengthy discussions with his reflection.

After what felt like hours but was probably only twenty minutes, during which we knocked on two wrong doors, we finally found ourselves in front of a modest two-story house set back from the street.

The house was well-maintained, with fresh paint in a soft yellow shade and crisp white trim. Winter-dormant flower beds lined the front walkway, their careful arrangement suggesting someone's dedicated attention during warmer months. The garage door was closed, but a kayak rack mounted on the side wall hinted at the family's maritime interests.

"At last," Ginger sighed as we approached the front door, his tail twitching with barely contained relief. "Your innovative approach to navigation has added several interesting detours to my mental map of the town."

The porch steps creaked slightly under my weight as I approached the door. A wind chime made of sea glass tinkled softly in the morning breeze, creating gentle music that seemed at odds with the tension I felt. The pieces caught the light, sending small rainbows dancing across the porch ceiling. The brass knocker was shaped like an anchor – a detail that seemed significant given what Ginger had noticed about our mystery woman's tattoo.

Several pairs of boots lined the porch wall, ranging from practical work boots to sailing shoes, all arranged with methodical precision. A coiled rope hung on a hook nearby, its precise knots suggesting someone familiar with nautical practices. Everything about the place spoke of order, routine, and attention to detail.

I knocked, the sound seeming unnaturally loud in the quiet street.

After a moment, heavy footsteps approached from inside, accompanied by the sound of multiple locks being undone. The door opened to reveal a man in his early fifties, his broad shoulders filling the doorframe. He wore a flannel shirt with the sleeves rolled up, revealing forearms corded with muscle. His hair was gray at the temples, deep laugh lines around his eyes suggested a naturally cheerful disposition, though there was no hint of that now.

"Can I help you?" His voice was deep but not unfriendly, though his eyes carried a wariness that suggested he already knew why I might be here. His stance in the doorway was protective, almost defensive.

"I'm looking for Alice," I said, noting how his expression shifted at his daughter's name. "Does she live here?"

The man's expression hardened, warmth replaced by something steelier. "You're Butterfield, aren't you? The private investigator?" His hand tightened on the doorframe, knuckles whitening slightly.

I nodded, watching how his posture had changed, becoming more protective. The transformation was subtle but significant – like a lighthouse beam switching from welcome to warning. "I'd like to ask Alice a few questions, if possible."

A woman appeared behind him – Alice's mother, unmistakably. She had the same red hair, the same delicate features that I'd seen in the bakery, though worry had drawn lines around her eyes that her daughter's face didn't yet show. She wore an apron with traces of flour, suggesting she shared her daughter's baking interests. Her hands twisted a dish towel anxiously, the fabric already wrinkled from repeated worrying.

"She's not talking to anyone right now," the father said firmly, shifting his stance to partially shield his wife from view. His hand tightened on the doorframe until I could see the tendons standing out. A muscle ticked in his jaw. "Especially not investigators."

I noticed a family photo on the wall behind them. Alice stood between her parents on what looked like a fishing boat, all three smiling. The contrast between that image and the defensive pair before me was striking.

"Sir, I understand your concern, but-"

"No, you don't understand," he cut me off. "My daughter is innocent. She's devastated about what happened to Liam, and she doesn't need people coming around asking accusations disguised as questions." His voice dropped lower, taking on an edge sharper than the winter wind. "She's been through enough. Leave her alone."

The mother's hands had stilled on the dish towel. She looked like she wanted to say something, but a slight head shake from her husband kept her silent. The family's unity was clear – they were circling the wagons, protecting their own.

"I'm afraid that's not possible," I tried again. "Given the circumstances-"

The door shut with enough force to make the sea glass wind chime shatter its gentle music into discordant notes. The sound echoed off the porch roof, mixing with the muffled voices I could hear arguing behind the closed door.

"Well," Ginger observed dryly, "that went about as well as your attempt to navigate here."

I knocked again, more insistently this time, but there was no response. Just silence broken only by the wind chime's now-settling music and the distant sound of a screen door slamming somewhere inside the house. A curtain twitched briefly in an upstairs window – Alice's room, perhaps? – but stayed firmly closed.

Behind that closed door lay answers – I was sure of it. The father's defensive posture, the mother's worried silence, that glimpse of movement upstairs – all pieces of a puzzle that was becoming more complex by the minute. The question was, how many more doors would close before we found them?

"You know," Ginger said as we made our way back down the porch steps, "for people claiming innocence, they're remarkably determined to avoid questions. Though I suppose having a private investigator show up on your doorstep just a couple hours after your daughter's boyfriend is found dead might put anyone in a defensive mood."

He had a point. The harbor breeze carried the distant sound of boat horns and seagulls, a reminder that somewhere out there, a killer walked free. Whether that killer was behind the door we'd just been shut out of remained to be seen.

# Chapter 9

"What now?" Ginger asked, delicately avoiding patches of slush as we walked. "I assume you have a plan that doesn't involve arguing with more locked doors or wrestling with that technological menace in your pocket."

I patted my coat where Sophie's note with Alice's address still sat alongside the crumpled photograph. "Actually, something Sophie said earlier keeps nagging at me. She mentioned Mrs. Abernathy recommending Alice for the bakery position. If she knew Alice well enough to suggest her for the job, she might know more about her background. We should pay Mrs. Abernathy a visit."

"Ah yes, our resident cookie connoisseur and keeper of town secrets," Ginger's tail lifted with interest. "Though I must say, the prospect of another encounter with her furry majesty, Mr. Whiskers, fills me with something less than enthusiasm."

The neighborhood streets were quiet, most people either at work or staying inside to avoid the bitter cold.

Patches of ice glinted treacherously on the sidewalk, forcing me to watch my step carefully.

"What do you make of Alice's parents?" I asked, remembering the father's protective stance, the mother's worried silence.

Ginger considered this as we navigated around a particularly treacherous patch of ice. "Their behavior was interesting. Protective, certainly, but not in the way guilty people usually are. More like…" He paused, whiskers twitching thoughtfully. "More like people who've had to protect before."

"I noticed that too," I nodded. "The father's stance in the doorway, the way he positioned himself between us and his wife – those weren't the actions of someone hiding a murderer. Those were the instincts of someone who's learned to guard against threats."

"Speaking of threats," Ginger added, "our friend Mike Sullivan seems to be hiding something rather significant beneath all that righteous fisherman indignation. Though how it all connects to our mystery woman from the docks remains to be seen."

We turned onto Maple Street, where Mrs. Abernathy had lived for as long as anyone in town could remember. Her Victorian house stood out among its neighbors, its gingerbread trim and wraparound porch meticulously maintained despite its age. The winter garden lay dormant now, but I knew that come spring, it would burst into carefully planned waves of color. Even the snow in her yard seemed neater somehow, as if it had arranged itself according to her exacting standards.

The scent of fresh-baked cookies wafted from somewhere inside, sweet and warm against the winter air. Smoke curled up from the chimney in precise ringlets, and through the front windows, I could see the warm glow of lamps against the early afternoon shadows.

"Well," Ginger observed as we approached the porch steps, "at least this visit promises better refreshments than our last investigation. Though I notice Mr. Whiskers has already assumed his observation post."

Sure enough, the massive gray Persian cat sat regally in the front window, his squashed face regarding us with his usual mix of disdain and territorial challenge. His fur seemed even more impressive than usual, as if he'd been recently groomed to maximum effect.

"Remember," I muttered as we reached the porch, "try to maintain diplomatic relations. We need information more than we need another feline border dispute."

"I shall endeavor to tolerate his imperial presence," Ginger replied loftily, though his tail had already begun to twitch.

The brass knocker echoed hollowly when I used it, but no response came from inside. The smell of baking grew stronger, suggesting Mrs. Abernathy was home but possibly distracted by her culinary pursuits. Through the window, Mr. Whiskers continued his silent judgment of our presence.

I knocked again, louder this time. After a moment, a faint "Oh dear!" floated through the door, followed by the sound of hurrying footsteps and what might have been a cookie sheet being set down rather hastily.

The door opened to release a wave of warm, cookie-scented air. Mrs. Abernathy stood there, flour dusting her silver hair and an apron that declared "Baking Is Love Made Visible" in elaborate embroidery. Her bright eyes widened with delight when she saw us.

"Mr. Butterfield! And Ginger too! Oh, your timing is perfect – I've just taken a batch of snickerdoodles out of the oven." She ushered us inside with the authority of someone used to being obeyed in matters of baked goods. "Come in, come in! Mind the rug – it's genuine Persian, just like Mr. Whiskers. Speaking of whom..."

Mr. Whiskers had descended from his window perch to assume a more strategic position on the back of an antique armchair. His massive tail curled around his paws with precise dignity as he studied us.

"Charmed, I'm sure," Ginger muttered, matching the Persian's regal posture with his own display of casual indifference. "Though I noticed your grooming seems a bit excessive for a simple afternoon at home. Expecting important company, are we?"

Mrs. Abernathy led us through her living room, where generations of doilies and carefully arranged knick-knacks testified to a lifetime of collecting. The walls were lined with photographs of the town's history – I spotted several featuring a younger Mrs. Abernathy at various community events, always impeccably dressed, always with a cat that bore a suspicious resemblance to Mr. Whiskers' ancestors perched nearby.

"Just let me get these cookies onto the cooling rack," she called over her shoulder as she disappeared into the kitchen. "Make yourselves comfortable! Mr. Whiskers, do be hospitable."

Mr. Whiskers' idea of hospitality apparently involved staring at Ginger with unblinking golden eyes while maintaining his position of tactical advantage on the armchair.

"I see your sophisticated understanding of personal space remains unchanged," Ginger observed dryly, settling onto a sunlit windowsill with deliberate casualness. "Though I must admit, your throne room is rather well-appointed. These curtains make excellent backdrop for properly dignified napping."

The kitchen clattered with the sounds of baking implements being rearranged. Mrs. Abernathy hummed as she worked, the tune something old and vaguely familiar. The house smelled of vanilla and cinnamon, with undertones of furniture polish and old books – the scent of a home that had been loved and maintained for decades.

"Now then," Mrs. Abernathy bustled back in, carrying a tray laden with cookies, tea things, and what appeared to be a small china saucer of cream. "Let's do this properly. Mr. Butterfield, you'll take milk with your tea? And Ginger, I haven't forgotten about you – this cream is from the local dairy farm, the good stuff."

She set about pouring tea with the precision of someone who'd elevated the action to an art form. Each movement was careful, practiced, perfect – from the angle of the teapot to the exact number of times she stirred each cup.

"Such attention to detail," Ginger commented, eyeing the cream saucer with clear approval. "Though I notice someone's portion appears significantly larger than mine." His gaze flicked to where Mr. Whiskers was delicately sampling from his own apparently larger saucer.

"Mrs. Abernathy," I began, accepting a teacup, "I wanted to ask you about Alice."

Her hands stilled briefly on the cookie plate. "Ah. I wondered if you might." She settled into her favorite armchair and smoothed her apron. "Such a terrible business, what happened to young Liam. The whole town's talking about it, of course. Though not everyone knows about Alice's connection to him."

"Sophie mentioned you recommended her for the bakery position," I said.

"Oh yes," she nodded, selecting a cookie with careful consideration. "I knew she'd be perfect for it. Such a gentle touch with pastry, and so eager to learn. When her parents asked me to teach her, I couldn't refuse."

"How did that come about?"

Mrs. Abernathy's face softened with remembrance. "Her parents came to me, oh, must be six or seven years ago now. Said Alice had a passion for baking but needed guidance. She was still in high school then, such a quiet thing. Spent weekends here, learning the proper way to cream butter, how to tell when a cake is done just by smell." She smiled, lost in memory. "We talked about everything while we baked – school, friends, boys she liked. Not Liam then, of course. He came later."

"You spent a lot of time with her," I observed, watching how Mr. Whiskers had begun a slow, dignified stalking maneuver along the back of the couch, gradually closing the distance to Ginger's windowsill. "Did you ever notice anything... unusual? Any signs of violence or aggressive tendencies?"

Mrs. Abernathy actually laughed, the sound bright against the tick of the grandfather clock in the corner. "Violence? Alice? Oh, Mr. Butterfield." She shook her head, silver curls bouncing. "That girl once spent an entire afternoon making a special batch of dog biscuits because she felt guilty about accidentally stepping on a puppy's tail at the park. The puppy hadn't even noticed, but Alice insisted on apologizing with baked goods."

"Your strategic advance isn't nearly as subtle as you imagine," Ginger commented to Mr. Whiskers, who had reduced the windowsill distance to approximately three feet. "But your ability to move that much fur with such calculated precision is almost impressive."

"Tell me about her during those baking lessons," I prompted, accepting another cookie. They were perfect –

crisp edges, soft centers, the ideal balance of cinnamon and sugar. No wonder Sophie had been trying to recreate Mrs. Abernathy's recipes.

"She was a natural," Mrs. Abernathy said, pouring more tea with practiced grace. "Not with the technical skills at first – those took time to develop. But she had the right instincts. Knew how to listen to the dough, if you understand what I mean. Some people try to force baking, to make it conform to their will. Alice understood that you have to work with it, let it tell you what it needs."

The afternoon light slanted through the windows, catching the delicate china tea set and making it gleam. Outside, a few snowflakes had begun to fall, dancing past the glass like tiny performers.

"She talked about everything while we baked," Mrs. Abernathy continued, lost in reminiscence. "Her dreams of maybe having her own café someday, her worry that she wasn't living up to her parents' expectations. She really liked Billy Patterson in her algebra class – this was long before Liam, of course. Used to blush every time she mentioned him." She smiled fondly. "We made special cookies when Billy asked someone else to the winter formal. Chocolate chip with extra chocolate – my recipe for broken hearts."

"Did she ever mention why she was so... nervous? The startling at loud noises, always watching the door?" I asked carefully.

Mrs. Abernathy's expression grew thoughtful. Her fingers traced the delicate pattern on her teacup. "Alice has always been sensitive – highly aware of her surroundings, you might say. Her mother was the same way at that age. It's not fear, exactly. More like... heightened perception. She notices everything, feels everything deeply." She paused, choosing her words with care. "Some people mistake that sensitivity for weakness. But in my experience, it's often the quiet ones who have the most strength."

"Speaking of strength," Ginger observed, "your regal companion appears to be preparing for some sort of tactical engagement. Though his battle strategy seems to consist mainly of aggressive grooming and meaningful stares."

Indeed, Mr. Whiskers had begun an elaborate grooming ritual, each stroke of his paw seeming to carry layers of significance. His golden eyes never left Ginger's position, even as he maintained an air of complete disinterest.

"The thing about Alice," Mrs. Abernathy continued, either oblivious to or choosing to ignore the feline power play unfolding in her living room, "is that she has this incredible capacity for gentleness. We once found a bird that had flown into the kitchen window during a lesson. Poor thing was just stunned, but Alice spent hours nursing it back to health. Made a little nest from one of my tea cozies, fed it water from an eyedropper. Wouldn't leave until she was sure it would recover."

The snow was falling more steadily now, adding another layer of quiet to the afternoon. The grandfather clock chimed three, its deep tones resonating through the house. Mr. Whiskers used the sound as cover to advance another few inches.

Mrs. Abernathy leaned forward in her chair, her voice dropping slightly. "I was there, you know, the day she met Liam. He came into my kitchen looking for his grandmother's old snickerdoodle recipe – apparently, she'd gotten it from me years ago. Alice was elbow-deep in bread dough, flour in her hair, completely focused on getting the kneading just right." She smiled at the memory. "The way he looked at her... like he'd walked into the kitchen expecting a recipe and found something much more valuable instead."

"Your attempt at nonchalant territorial expansion continues to be obvious," Ginger commented to Mr. Whiskers, who had somehow managed to reduce the windowsill distance to mere inches while maintaining an air of complete indifference. "Though I must commend your commitment to appearing entirely focused on that imaginary dust speck you've been studying for the past five minutes."

"Did she change after meeting Liam?" I asked, watching how Mrs. Abernathy's hands moved constantly as she spoke – adjusting a doily, straightening a teacup, small precise movements that seemed to help her organize her thoughts.

"At first, she bloomed," Mrs. Abernathy said, her expression softening. "Like a flower finally finding the right amount of sunlight. Liam shared her love of the ocean, you see. They'd spend hours on his rental boats, just talking about marine life and conservation. He taught her about different species of fish, she taught him about the perfect ratio of butter to flour in a pie crust." She paused, something darker flickering across her face. "But lately…"

"Lately?" I prompted gently.

She sighed, the sound barely audible over the tick of the grandfather clock. "Lately, she seemed to withdraw. Started missing our usual baking sessions. When she did come, she was distracted, jumpy. Not afraid, exactly, but… worried. Like she was carrying something heavy but couldn't put it down."

The snow continued to fall outside, creating a soft white curtain beyond the windows. The afternoon light had taken on that peculiar winter quality – bright but somehow distant, like it was being filtered through layers of memory.

"Your strategic position may be superior," Ginger noted to Mr. Whiskers, who had finally claimed the far end of the windowsill, "but I feel compelled to point out that your left whisker is slightly askew. Most unseemly for a cat of your supposed breeding."

Mr. Whiskers' response was a slight twitch of said whisker, though whether in acknowledgment or disdain was unclear.

"The last time I saw her – must have been about a week ago," Mrs. Abernathy continued, absently rearranging the cookies on their plate into perfect concentric circles. "She seemed... different. Not scared, exactly, but determined. Like someone who's made a difficult decision and is trying to live with it." She looked up at me, her bright eyes sharp behind her glasses. "She's not capable of violence, Mr. Butterfield. I know everyone in this town has secrets – goodness knows I've heard most of them over tea and cookies through the years. But Alice? That girl couldn't hurt anyone. She still apologizes to cookie dough if she kneads it too firmly."

Something about Mrs. Abernathy's certainty, the way she spoke about Alice – it carried the weight of years of observation, of countless hours spent in quiet conversation over mixing bowls and cooling racks. The Alice she described seemed impossible to reconcile with someone capable of murder.

# Chapter 10

"May I ask you something personal?" I said, setting down my teacup. The delicate china made a soft sound against its saucer. "Why did you never open your own bakery? From what I've heard, you could have given Maggie serious competition."

Mrs. Abernathy's face softened into a fond smile as she reached down to adjust her apron. "Gregg – my late husband – asked me the same thing, years ago. But you see, Mr. Butterfield, baking isn't just about the end product. It's about the process, the love that goes into it. The moment you turn it into a business, something changes." She gestured around her kitchen, where copper pots gleamed and spice jars stood in perfect alphabetical order. "Here, I can bake what I want, when I want, for whom I want. Every cookie has a story, every pie a purpose."

"Your philosophical approach to territorial sovereignty continues to fascinate," Ginger observed as Mr. Whiskers executed a perfectly timed stretch that somehow managed to occupy exactly one more inch of windowsill. "But your dedication to appearing casually disinterested while systematically invading my space shows impressive commitment."

"That's why I understood Alice so well," Mrs. Abernathy continued, her fingers tracing the delicate pattern on her teacup. "She has that same sensitivity to the process. When she bakes, it's not just about following a recipe – it's about putting something of herself into every creation. That's not something you can teach. It's either in your heart or it isn't."

The grandfather clock chimed the quarter-hour, its deep tones resonating through the house. Outside, the snow had begun to fall more heavily, creating a hushed backdrop to our conversation. The midafternoon light filtered through the curtains, casting long shadows across the immaculate living room.

"Did she ever talk about Liam's environmental work?" I asked, accepting another cookie.

"Oh yes, especially in the beginning. She was so proud of his dedication to marine conservation." Mrs. Abernathy's expression clouded slightly. "But lately, when his name came up, she'd get this look – like someone trying to solve a particularly difficult puzzle. The last time she mentioned him..." She trailed off, lost in thought.

"The last time?" I prompted gently.

"It was different," she said slowly, her hands automatically straightening an already perfectly aligned doily. "She seemed worried, but not for herself. It was more like... like when you know someone you care about is heading down a dangerous path, but you can't figure out how to stop them."

"Your attempts at subtle intimidation would be more effective," Ginger commented to Mr. Whiskers, "if you hadn't just knocked that dust mote off your nose in what I can only describe as a distinctly undignified manner."

The Persian's only response was to begin another round of meticulous grooming, though his golden eyes never left Ginger's position.

"Alice has a gentle soul," Mrs. Abernathy said firmly, setting her teacup down with a decisive clink. "Whatever happened to Liam – and mind you, I have my own theories about that – she couldn't have done it. That girl still cries over sad commercials and spends her tip money buying food for stray cats."

The certainty in her voice, combined with everything she'd shared about Alice, painted a picture very different from what I'd initially imagined. The quiet young woman I'd observed in the bakery, always watching the door, starting at loud noises – perhaps I'd been reading those signs all wrong.

"Your insight into her character seems quite thorough," I observed, watching how Mrs. Abernathy's eyes constantly tracked everything in her environment – a trait, I realized, that reminded me of Alice's own heightened awareness.

"When you spend as many hours as we did, talking over mixing bowls and cooling racks, you get to know someone's true nature," she replied, reaching down to adjust her already perfectly straight apron. "Alice isn't hiding anything dark, Mr. Butterfield."

The snow continued to fall outside, creating a soft white curtain that muffled the occasional passing car. The afternoon light had taken on that peculiar winter quality – bright but somehow distant.

I set my teacup down, considering everything Mrs. Abernathy had shared about Alice. While it painted a clear picture of her character, I realized I knew very little about the victim himself. "We've talked a lot about Alice, but what about Liam? Is there someone in town who knew him well? His parents perhaps?"

A shadow crossed Mrs. Abernathy's face. "His parents died in a car crash when he was just a boy. He was raised by his grandmother – Margaret. Strict woman, but fair. She passed away two years ago." She adjusted a cookie on the plate, her movements precise. "I knew Margaret well – she used to come by for tea every Wednesday. But Liam... he was always polite when I saw him. We didn't talk much – our paths just didn't cross often outside of those brief hellos when he'd stop by to see his grandmother."

"Anyone else who might have known him better?"

"Well," Mrs. Abernathy brightened slightly, "Margaret used to mention how well he did in biology class. He had a natural talent for it, she said. Ms. Chambers – that's the biology teacher at the high school – she took him under her wing. Still teaches there, actually. She's probably at school now, grading papers. She always stays late this time of year." She nodded decisively. "Wonderful woman, Ms. Chambers. If anyone can tell you about Liam's character, it would be her."

"Your conversation about potential witnesses is fascinating," Ginger observed to Mr. Whiskers, "though I couldn't help but notice your strategic retreat to the armchair coincided perfectly with that last gust of cold air through the window."

"You mentioned having theories about what happened to Liam," I said carefully, watching her face. "Care to share them?"

Mrs. Abernathy's eyes flickered briefly to the window, where the falling snow had begun to accumulate on the sill, creating a delicate white barrier between Mr. Whiskers and Ginger. "In a town this size, Mr. Butterfield, everyone has theories. And everyone has secrets they'd rather keep buried." She paused, selecting another cookie with deliberate care. "But sometimes, when people try to expose those secrets, things get... complicated."

"I see your strategic accumulation of snow has provided an unexpected tactical advantage," Ginger observed to Mr. Whiskers, who had been forced to retreat slightly from the cold windowsill. "Though I must say, nature's intervention in our territorial dispute seems rather heavy-handed."

Mrs. Abernathy rose to adjust the thermostat. The radiator clanked to life, its gentle hiss adding another layer to the afternoon's quiet symphony. "You know, Mr. Butterfield, I've lived in this town long enough to see patterns. The way certain people react when their comfortable routines are threatened. The lengths they'll go to protect what they consider theirs."

She returned to her chair, smoothing her skirt with practiced efficiency. "Alice isn't the one you should be worried about. That girl wears her heart on her sleeve – always has. It's the ones who seem the most righteous, the most indignant about Liam's activities… those are the ones worth watching."

The grandfather clock struck four, its deep tones seeming to emphasize the weight of her words. Outside, the snow had begun to coat the street in earnest, transforming Oceanview Cove into something from a winter postcard – beautiful on the surface, but hiding whatever secrets lay beneath its white blanket.

"Your meteorological retreat is noted," Ginger commented to Mr. Whiskers, who had settled for a strategic position on a nearby armchair. "Though I suspect this temporary ceasefire is more about preserving your dignity than admitting defeat."

I found myself thinking back to Mike Sullivan's bandaged hand, his defensive posture at the café. To the mysterious woman slipping out of Liam's rental shack during the protest. To Alice's father, standing guard in his doorway like someone who'd learned the hard way about protecting what he loved.

The pieces were there, but they still wouldn't quite fit together. Yet something Mrs. Abernathy had said struck a chord – about people protecting what they considered theirs. About secrets worth killing for.

"Thank you," I said, rising from my chair. The tea had gone cold, but the warmth of understanding had begun to replace my earlier suspicions. "You've given me a lot to think about."

"Just remember," Mrs. Abernathy said, walking us to the door. Her silver hair caught the late afternoon light, creating a halo effect that seemed appropriate for someone who'd spent decades observing and understanding her neighbors. "Sometimes the most obvious solution isn't the right one. And sometimes, the quiet ones are quiet for a reason."

She pressed a small paper bag into my hands – more cookies, still warm. "For the investigation," she said with a knowing smile. "I've found that most problems look different after a proper snack."

"Your hospitality has been noted," Ginger said to Mr. Whiskers, who had resumed his window post with regal dignity. "Though I feel compelled to point out that your human's baking skills far exceed your abilities as a strategic opponent."

As we stepped out into the snowy afternoon, I found my earlier suspicions about Alice beginning to fade, replaced by new questions. If she wasn't behind Liam's death, what was she trying to protect? And more importantly, who was she trying to protect it from?

The snow continued to fall, each flake carrying its own small secret to add to the growing blanket of white that covered Oceanview Cove. Somewhere in this town, someone had killed Liam. But increasingly, I was beginning to think we'd been looking in the wrong direction.

"Well," Ginger said as we made our way carefully down the snow-covered sidewalk, "at least this visit was more productive than our last investigation. Though I must say, Mr. Whiskers' territorial posturing lacks the subtle finesse one expects from a cat of his supposed breeding."

"Productive?" I raised an eyebrow at my feline partner. "From what I observed, you were too busy engaging in cold war tactics over windowsill real estate to do much investigating."

"I'll have you know that my strategic engagement with Mr. Whiskers was purely for investigative purposes," Ginger sniffed, delicately avoiding a patch of ice. "One must maintain certain professional standards when dealing with self-appointed feline aristocracy. Though I must admit, his tactical retreat to the armchair was rather satisfying. Besides, I noticed plenty while defending my position. Like how convinced Mrs. Abernathy was about Alice's character."

I reached into the bag for another cookie, considering his words. The snickerdoodle was still warm, its cinnamon-sugar coating crystallized perfectly. "She did paint quite a different picture of Alice than what we've seen. The nervous girl at the bakery seems hard to reconcile with someone who spends hours nursing injured birds."

"Unless," Ginger pointed out, his tail swishing thoughtfully through the falling snow, "her nervousness comes from something else entirely. Something she's trying to protect, as Mrs. Abernathy suggested. Though I notice you seem less convinced she's our killer now."

"It's hard to imagine someone who apologizes to cookie dough committing murder," I admitted, brushing snow from my sleeve. "But that still leaves us with more questions than answers."

The snow crunched under my boots as we turned onto Main Street. A school bus passed by, its yellow bulk bright against the white landscape, reminding me of Mrs. Abernathy's suggestion about Ms. Chambers. Through the swirling snow, children's laughter echoed from a nearby yard where they were building a snowman.

"That officer at the docks," I said slowly, watching the kids play, "the one who suggested suicide... maybe we shouldn't dismiss it entirely. Sometimes the people who seem happiest on the surface..."

Ginger's whiskers twitched with amusement. "My, my. Are we actually considering theories from Miller's crack investigative team? The same people who thought that Christmas tree incident was a simple electrical malfunction? Next you'll be telling me you trust their judgment about proper donut selection."

"I know, I know. But if we could talk to Ms. Chambers, learn more about Liam's character..." I paused, brushing snow from my coat. "Mike Sullivan's bizarre behavior, that mysterious woman at the rental shack – they're still part of this puzzle. But if there were signs, hints of depression or suicidal tendencies in Liam's past... well, it wouldn't be the first time someone's passion for a cause masked deeper struggles."

"The high school's just ahead," Ginger observed as we approached the imposing brick building. Its windows glowed warmly against the gathering dusk, suggesting that Mrs. Abernathy had been right about teachers working late. Light spilled from the second-floor windows, creating golden rectangles on the fresh snow. "Though I do hope this interview proves more substantive than your previous attempts at gathering information. My diplomatic skills can only handle so many territorial disputes in one day. And I notice a distinct lack of Persian cats in the vicinity, which already improves our investigative prospects."

"At least we got cookies out of the last interview," I said, patting the paper bag in my pocket.

As we reached the school gates, I found myself thinking about everything Mrs. Abernathy had shared. We'd learned plenty about Alice, but Liam himself remained a mystery – the passionate environmentalist, the orphan raised by his grandmother, the biology student who'd found his calling in marine conservation. Time to fill in those blanks.

# Chapter 11

The high school loomed before us in the gathering dusk, its red brick facade darkened by the falling snow. Most of the windows were already dark, but a few squares of warm light spilled onto the fresh snow, creating golden patterns that seemed to hover between earth and sky. The building had that peculiar institutional design common to schools built in the 1960s – functional rather than beautiful, but somehow dignified in its simplicity.

The main entrance was flanked by concrete planters where, in warmer months, students maintained a small garden as part of their biology projects. Now they held only snow, pristine and untouched, like blank pages waiting to be written on.

"Well," Ginger observed as we approached the front doors, shaking snow from his paws with fastidious care, "the institutional architecture leaves something to be desired. Would it have killed them to include a few strategic sunbathing spots?"

The security guard sat at a desk just inside the entrance, his blue uniform neat but clearly worn comfortable with age, like a favorite book that's been read many times. The nameplate on his desk read "Henry Sullivan" – no relation to Mike, I assumed, though in a town this size, you never knew. I recognized him from the Salty Breeze, where we'd exchanged polite nods a few times over the past months, though we'd never really talked. He looked up from his crossword puzzle as we entered, recognition lighting his face.

"Mr. Butterfield!" He set down his pencil, genuine warmth in his greeting. His mustache, shot through with gray, twitched as he smiled. "Heard you might be looking into what happened to young Liam. Terrible business, that. Just terrible."

The lobby smelled of floor wax and chalk dust, that peculiar combination unique to schools that somehow persists despite modern cleaning products. A trophy case along one wall displayed various academic and athletic achievements, the glass slightly foggy with age but meticulously clean. A newer plaque caught my eye – an environmental science award with Liam's name engraved on it.

"Hello, Mr. Sullivan," I replied, brushing snow from my coat. "I didn't realize you worked here."

He chuckled, the sound echoing slightly in the empty lobby. "Going on fifteen years now. Watch these kids grow up, graduate, some come back with their own little ones." His expression sobered. "Watched Liam grow up too. Smart kid. Maybe too smart for his own good, in the end."

"Actually, I'm looking for Ms. Chambers," I said. "I heard she might be able to tell me more about Liam's school days."

Henry nodded, checking his ancient flip phone for the time. "Cora? Yeah, she's still here. Always stays late this time of year, grading papers and setting up lab experiments. Second floor, room 214." He pointed toward the main staircase, its rubber treads worn smooth by generations of students.

The stairs creaked slightly under our feet as we climbed, the sound seeming unnaturally loud in the empty building. Trophy cases lined the walls, their contents catching the emergency lights' dim glow. More environmental awards, I noticed, several bearing Liam's name.

Ms. Chambers sat at her desk, surrounded by stacks of papers and what appeared to be carefully labeled specimen jars. She was younger than I'd expected, probably in her early forties, with dark hair pulled back in a practical ponytail and wire-rimmed glasses that caught the light as she looked up at our approach. Her navy cardigan had patches on the elbows – not from wear, I realized, but sewn on purposefully, giving her a deliberately academic appearance.

"Can I help you?" Her voice was warm but tired, suggesting long hours of grading papers. A half-empty coffee mug sat beside her, bearing the faded logo of some past science conference.

"Ms. Chambers? I'm Jim Butterfield. I was hoping to talk to you about Liam Taylor."

Her hands stilled on the papers she'd been grading, red pen hovering above what looked like a diagram of cell division. A wave of sadness washed over her face, the genuine grief of a teacher who'd lost a promising student.

"Oh, Liam..." She removed her glasses, rubbing the bridge of her nose. "I've been trying to focus on grading these papers, but I keep thinking about him. Such a waste. So much potential, so much passion..."

I pulled up a nearby student chair, its legs scraping softly against the linoleum floor. The room smelled of dry-erase markers and that particular scent unique to science classrooms – a mixture of cleaning supplies and preserved specimens.

"I brought cookies," I said, offering the bag from Mrs. Abernathy. "Still warm."

A small smile touched her lips as she accepted one. "Mrs. Abernathy's snickerdoodles. She hasn't changed her recipe in twenty years, thank goodness." She took a bite, closing her eyes briefly. "Liam used to sneak these into my classroom during lunch period. Said they helped him think better during afternoon labs."

The classroom itself seemed frozen in mid-lesson. Half-finished diagrams covered the whiteboard, and a model of DNA spiral hung from the ceiling, slowly rotating in the air currents from the heating vent. Posters of marine ecosystems lined the walls, their corners curling slightly with age.

"You taught him biology?" I prompted gently.

"For three years." She straightened in her chair, and I could see memories surfacing. "I remember his first day in my class like it was yesterday. Most freshmen come in nervous, unsure. Not Liam. He walked straight to the front row, pulled out this battered copy of Jacques Cousteau's 'The Silent World' – clearly read multiple times – and asked if we'd be covering marine ecosystems."

She smiled at the memory, reaching for another cookie. "By the end of that first week, he'd already started a petition to add an advanced marine biology course to the curriculum. Didn't get it, of course, but that was Liam – always thinking bigger, always pushing for more."

"Sounds like he knew his path early," I observed.

"Oh yes, though it wasn't always easy." She gestured to a shelf lined with specimen jars. "See that collection? Liam started that in his sophomore year. Spent every weekend collecting samples from tide pools, cataloging species, tracking changes in populations. The other kids teased him at first – called him 'Fish Boy', tried to knock his samples over in the hallway."

"How did he handle that?"

Ms. Chambers sighed, adjusting a stack of papers on her desk. "Not well, initially. Liam had this... intensity about him. When he believed in something, he believed with his whole heart. And if you challenged those beliefs..." She shook her head. "There were fights. Nothing too serious – mostly shoving matches in the hallway. But he had trouble controlling his temper when people dismissed his environmental concerns."

"What changed?"

"The science fair in his junior year." She stood, moving to a bulletin board covered with photographs. "Here – this was the project that turned everything around."

The photo showed a younger Liam standing proudly beside an elaborate display. Charts and graphs covered the boards, along with underwater photographs and detailed drawings of marine life.

"He spent months on that project," Ms. Chambers continued, her voice warm with pride. "Documented how agricultural runoff was affecting local marine ecosystems. Real research, college-level work. Even the kids who used to tease him had to admit it was impressive. He won first place, went on to the state competition."

"The enthusiasm of youth," Ginger observed quietly from his perch on a nearby chair, his tone unusually gentle.

"But it wasn't just academic for him, was it?" I asked.

"No," she replied, returning to her desk. "Liam felt everything deeply. The oceans weren't just an ecosystem to study – they were something to protect, to fight for. His grandmother, Margaret, used to worry that he'd burn himself out. But that passion... it was just who he was."

She picked up a framed photograph from her desk, studying it for a moment before passing it to me. It showed a group of students in lab coats, gathered around a dissection table. Liam stood in the center, gesturing animatedly about something.

"This was his AP Biology class. He'd organized a special unit on marine conservation. See how engaged everyone is? That was Liam's gift – he could make others care as much as he did. When he talked about ocean acidification or overfishing, you couldn't help but listen. He made it personal, made it matter."

"Ms. Chambers," I said carefully, "I need to ask something difficult. In all your time teaching him, did you ever notice any signs of depression? Any indication that he might have had... darker thoughts?"

Her response was immediate and emphatic. "Absolutely not." She set down the photo with gentle precision. "Liam faced his share of challenges – losing his parents so young, being raised by his grandmother, the constant battles to be taken seriously. But he never lost his drive, his sense of purpose. If anything, those challenges made him more determined."

She paused, choosing her words carefully. "Two days before... before it happened... I ran into him in the town square. He was practically vibrating with excitement, told me he'd gathered some new evidence about fishing quotas. Said he was finally going to make real change happen." Her voice caught slightly. "That's what I keep coming back to. He was so alive, so full of plans. He talked about future projects, about making a difference. That's not someone looking to end things – that's someone looking forward to what comes next."

Her words aligned perfectly with what Dylan had told me during the protest – about Liam's phone call, about having evidence that made him nervous. Whatever Liam had discovered in those final days, it had been significant enough to excite him but dangerous enough to make him cautious. The timing couldn't be coincidental.

"Tell me more about his school days," I prompted, filing away this connection for later consideration. "What else stands out in your memories?"

Ms. Chambers leaned back in her chair, absently turning a pencil between her fingers. "He had this habit of turning every assignment into an environmental statement. Once, for a genetics unit, most students did projects on inherited traits in their families. Liam? He did a detailed analysis of genetic diversity in local fish populations and how overfishing was creating evolutionary bottlenecks."

She smiled, shaking her head. "I had to give him extra credit just for the sheer ambition of it. That was typical Liam – never taking the easy path if there was a chance to make a larger point."

"Did his grandmother support his interests?"

"Margaret? Oh yes, though sometimes I think she worried about how all-consuming it was. She'd come to parent-teacher conferences, this tiny, fierce woman with perfect posture, always asking if Liam was balancing his passion with other interests." Ms. Chambers reached for another cookie. "She was strict with him, but in a good way. Gave him structure when he needed it most."

The heating system kicked on with a mechanical groan, sending the DNA model into a lazy spin. Outside the windows, snow continued to fall, creating an oddly peaceful backdrop to our conversation.

"There was this incident his senior year," Ms. Chambers continued, her expression growing more serious. "Some boys were messing around with chemicals in the lab, poured something toxic down the drain. Liam caught them at it. Could have just reported it to me, but instead, he confronted them directly. Ended up in quite a scuffle – gave one boy a bloody nose, got a black eye himself."

"Sounds serious," I observed.

"It was, but not in the way you might think. Instead of just punishing everyone involved, the principal made them all work together on an environmental impact project. Liam turned it into this whole study of how chemical waste affects marine life. By the end of it, those same boys were helping him organize beach cleanups."

She stood, moving to adjust a crooked poster of the ocean food chain. "That was Liam's real gift – not just the passion, but the ability to make others share it. Even when his methods were... impulsive."

The classroom had grown darker as we talked, the winter evening pressing against the windows. The snow outside created an odd, diffused glow, making the room feel somehow separate from the rest of the world.

"You know what I keep thinking about?" Ms. Chambers said softly, returning to her desk. "His last project here. Senior year, he organized this whole campaign about plastic pollution in the harbor. Got the whole school involved – art students making posters, math classes calculating waste volumes, English classes writing letters to local businesses."

She opened a drawer, pulling out what looked like a student newspaper. The front page showed Liam standing on the beach, surrounded by fellow students all holding trash bags.

"He could have just done the minimum required for graduation. Instead, he turned it into this whole movement. That was Liam – always seeing the bigger picture, always pushing for more." She looked up at me, her eyes bright with unshed tears. "That's why I can't accept that he would... that he could..."

"Take his own life?" I finished gently.

"No," she said firmly. "Never. Liam was a fighter. Even when things were hard – and they often were – he never gave up. He'd just find another angle, another way to make his point."

She carefully returned the newspaper to its drawer. "The world needs people like that, Mr. Butterfield. People who care so much they won't back down, even when it would be easier. Liam was going to make a difference. He already was."

"Thank you," I said, standing. The student chair creaked as I pushed it back. "You've helped clear up some important questions."

Ms. Chambers nodded, her hands automatically straightening papers that were already neat. "Just... find out what really happened to him, Mr. Butterfield. Liam deserves that much."

"I'll do my best," I promised softly, meaning it. "We'll figure out the truth."

As we made our way back through the darkened hallways, our footsteps echoing in the empty building, I found my earlier questions about suicide fading completely. The Liam that Ms. Chambers had described – passionate, determined, absolutely certain of his path – matched the young man I'd observed at the Salty Breeze. Someone that focused, that sure of their purpose, doesn't simply give up.

"Well," Ginger said quietly as we emerged into the snowy evening, "I believe we can safely rule out certain theories. But it makes our remaining possibilities significantly more troubling."

The school loomed behind us, its windows now almost entirely dark except for Ms. Chambers' room, where light still spilled onto the fresh snow. The flakes had begun to fall more heavily, transforming the mundane school parking lot into something almost ethereal. Our footprints from earlier had already been filled in, as if erasing evidence of our passage.

The image of young Liam from the photographs stayed with me – the passionate student with his marine biology projects, the determined environmentalist in the making, the fighter who turned enemies into allies. It painted a picture so different from what some people in town had been suggesting. Not a troublemaker, but a crusader. Not depressed, but driven.

"Our teacher provided quite a different perspective on our victim," Ginger observed, delicately picking his way through the snow.

"She did," I agreed, pulling my coat tighter against the cold. The wind had picked up, carrying the sharp bite of winter. "Someone that focused, that determined... Suicide just doesn't fit."

"Which leaves us with more concerning alternatives," Ginger noted, pausing to shake snow from his paws. "Though I notice our list of potential suspects seems to grow with each conversation. Quite the talent our young environmentalist had for making enemies while trying to make the world better."

The street lights had come on, creating pools of yellow light in the gathering darkness. Each one was surrounded by a halo of falling snow, like tiny spotlights illuminating scenes in a play where we still didn't know all the actors.

"The Salty Breeze?" I suggested. "We could use some time to think this through. Maybe share what we've learned with the others."

"Assuming you can navigate there without consulting your technological nemesis," Ginger agreed.

We walked in companionable silence through the falling snow, each lost in our own thoughts. The Liam who had emerged from Ms. Chambers' memories seemed more complex than the angry environmentalist from the bar – passionate but focused, determined but not destructive. Someone whose convictions might make enemies, but not someone who would give up on his cause.

Which meant, of course, that someone had killed him. Someone who had felt threatened enough by his investigations, his evidence gathering, his relentless pursuit of what he saw as right, to take drastic action. And that someone was still out there, probably watching our investigation with growing concern.

The lights of the Salty Breeze appeared through the swirling snow, warm and inviting. Maybe our friends would have new insights to share, new pieces to add to this increasingly complex puzzle. At the very least, we could use their perspectives – and, if I was being honest, one of Shawn's special cocktails wouldn't hurt either.

The wind picked up as we approached the bar, carrying the mixed scents of snow and sea. Somewhere in the darkness, waves crashed against the shore, their rhythm as constant as the questions that still needed answers. Questions that seemed to multiply with every new piece of information we uncovered.

It was time to share what we'd learned, to put all our pieces on the table and see what pattern emerged. Time to review all of today's revelations with friends who might see something we'd missed.

# Chapter 12

The Salty Breeze's warmth enveloped us as we stepped inside, a welcome contrast to the snowy evening. The familiar scents of polished wood, beer, and Shawn's latest experimental cocktail creation wrapped around us like a comfortable blanket. The ancient jukebox in the corner was playing something soft and jazzy – Nina Simone, I thought, though the speakers' age made it hard to be certain.

Shawn stood behind the counter, methodically polishing glasses with the focused precision of someone who'd turned the simple act into an art form. Robert occupied his regular seat, nursing his usual dark beer, while Emma had arranged an impressive array of crystals around her drink in what she probably considered the optimal configuration for cosmic energy absorption.

"There's our intrepid investigators!" Shawn called out as we approached, already reaching for the ingredients of my usual Librarian cocktail. His checked shirt was rolled up to the elbows, showing forearms strong from years of breaking up bar fights and carrying kegs. "Was beginning to think you'd gotten lost in all this snow."

"Nearly did," I admitted, settling onto my familiar barstool. The leather was worn smooth from years of faithful service, molded perfectly to accommodate regular patrons. "Though I blame Emma's technological improvements to my phone. That GPS has a rather creative interpretation of local geography."

Emma brightened, her numerous bangles creating a symphony of tiny chimes as she turned toward me. Today she wore what appeared to be a dress made entirely of constellation patterns, complete with tiny LED stars that twinkled when she moved. "Oh! Did the celestial navigation app help? I specially programmed it to align with Mercury's current position."

"Is that why it tried to direct me through Mrs. Henderson's backyard?" I asked dryly. "Something about optimal cosmic routing?"

"The stars work in mysterious ways," Emma said serenely, adjusting a particularly large crystal that seemed to be acting as a paperweight for what looked like a hand-drawn star chart. "Though I should mention that Mercury is currently in retrograde, which can affect electronic communications. Did you get Aaron's call earlier? I might have mentioned something about the case when he asked about your new phone..."

"Ah yes," Ginger commented, claiming his usual spot beside me. "Our impromptu video chat adventure. Jim's ceiling fan gave quite a compelling performance during his technological gymnastics."

"Yes, about that," I turned to Emma, watching as Shawn crafted my cocktail with practiced efficiency. "Any particular reason you felt the need to inform Aaron about our latest case?"

Emma's bangles jingled as she waved her hands in what might have been explanation or an attempt to realign cosmic forces. "The stars indicated it was an auspicious time for information sharing! Besides, Lily was asking about you. She's doing much better in school now, you know. No more treasure hunting adventures."

"Unlike some people," Robert muttered into his beer, "who seem to find trouble without even looking for it."

Shawn set my finished cocktail in front of me with a flourish. The amber liquid caught the bar's warm light, creating patterns that would probably have Emma expounding on celestial significance. "Give Jim a break," he said, though his eyes twinkled with amusement. "At least this case doesn't involve mechanical elves or holiday-themed death traps."

"No, just murder, protests, and mysterious women with anchor tattoos," I said, taking a sip of my drink. Shawn had outdone himself – the balance of flavors was perfect, warming without being overwhelming. "Speaking of which..."

I quickly filled them in on everything we'd learned – about Alice's true character from Mrs. Abernathy, about

Liam's passionate nature from Ms. Chambers, about the mysterious woman at the rental shack. The bar's usual evening sounds provided a backdrop to my narrative – the clink of glasses, the murmur of conversations at distant tables, the occasional burst of laughter from a group of regulars in the corner.

"An anchor tattoo, you say?" Robert's face creased in thought as he turned his beer mug between calloused hands. "Lots of those around here. Sailors, fishermen's daughters, tourists thinking it makes them look nautical."

"Yes, but combined with knowing the docks well enough to navigate them during a protest?" I pointed out. "That suggests someone local, someone comfortable around boats."

"Speaking of locals," Shawn said, lowering his voice as he leaned in over the bar. His expression had grown serious, the lines around his eyes deepening. "I've noticed something odd these past few days. The fishermen who come in – the regulars, you know? They're different."

"Different how?" I asked, watching as he automatically wiped an already clean spot on the bar.

"Quieter. More cautious." Shawn glanced around before continuing. "Usually, they're a rowdy bunch – arguing about sports, bragging about catches, that sort of thing. But lately? They huddle in corners, speaking in whispers. And they watch the door like they're expecting trouble."

"Like that group over there," Emma interjected, gesturing discreetly with a crystal-laden hand toward a table in the corner. Three fishermen I recognized as regulars sat hunched over their beers, their conversation barely audible despite the bar's relative quiet. They kept glancing toward the entrance, their postures tense.

"Exactly," Shawn nodded. "Been like that since Liam died. Something's got them spooked."

Robert set down his beer, the mug making a soft but definitive sound against the wooden bar. "Might have something to do with what I heard today," he said, his voice dropping even lower. The bar lights caught the silver in his beard as he leaned forward. "There's talk among the fleet. Rumors, mostly, but..."

He paused, seeming to weigh his words carefully. The jukebox had moved on to Billie Holiday, her melancholic voice a fitting accompaniment to the growing tension in our small group.

"Mike Sullivan's crew," Robert continued finally. "Word is they've been exceeding quotas. Not by a little, either. And Liam... word is he had proof."

"Well," Ginger observed dryly from his spot beside me, "that would certainly explain our friend Mike's rather aggressive reaction to environmental activism. Though his bandaged wrist suggests a rather unsubtle approach to problem-solving."

"That's not all," Robert added, absently turning his mug between weathered fingers. "Danny Richards – he runs the 'Morning Star' out of the north dock – he saw something the night Liam died. Didn't think much of it at the time, but now..."

We all leaned in closer, creating a small island of conspiracy in the bar's warm atmosphere. Even Emma's crystals seemed to still their usual dancing movements in her jewelry.

"Danny was coming in late, taking the long way around the harbor because of the ice. Says he saw a boat heading out – one of the rental types, like Liam used. Two people on board, man and woman from what he could make out. But it was dark, and he was pretty far off."

"The stars did indicate a masculine and feminine energy intertwined with tragedy that night," Emma added, her voice carrying that dreamy quality it took on when she was channeling her celestial insights. "Neptune's influence was particularly strong."

"Did Danny recognize either person?" I asked, mentally adding this new piece to our growing puzzle.

Robert shook his head. "Too far, too dark. Just saw the silhouettes against the running lights. Could've been anyone. Danny didn't think anything of it until the next morning when..." He trailed off, taking another sip of beer.

"When they found Liam in the nets," I finished quietly.

The bar seemed to grow quieter around us, though objectively I knew the ambient noise hadn't changed. The jukebox had moved on to something more upbeat, creating an odd contrast with our somber conversation.

"The thing is," Shawn said, automatically reaching for a glass to polish, "if Liam had evidence about fishing quotas, where is it now? The police searched his rental shack, right?"

"Not very thoroughly, knowing Miller," Robert grunted. "Man couldn't find a fish in an aquarium."

"But someone else was looking," I reminded them, thinking of the mysterious woman I'd glimpsed through the window. "And she found something – papers, documents, something she thought worth taking during the chaos of the protest."

Emma's bangles created a gentle chiming as she rearranged her crystals into what was presumably a more cosmically advantageous configuration. "The stars suggest hidden truths coming to light," she said thoughtfully. "Though Mercury's retrograde position does indicate some confusion about who can be trusted."

"For once," Ginger commented from his perch, "Emma's celestial predictions align remarkably well with earthly events. Though I suspect that has more to do with the inherent sketchiness of several suspects than any planetary influence."

The evening crowd had begun to filter in more steadily now, bringing with them bursts of cold air and the scent of snow each time the door opened. The regular rhythm of the bar continued around us – Shawn occasionally breaking away to serve customers, the clink of glasses, the low murmur of conversations, the gentle crackle of the fireplace fighting back the winter chill.

"What about Alice?" Emma asked, her voice soft but intent. "The cards – I did a reading this morning – they suggest a young woman caught between love and duty."

"Alice…" I considered everything we'd learned about her – Mrs. Abernathy's stories of her gentleness, her nervousness at the bakery, her parents' fierce protectiveness. "It's hard to imagine her involved in something like this. The way Mrs. Abernathy described her…"

"People can surprise you," Robert pointed out gruffly. "Look at Maggie."

"True," Ginger observed, his tail twitching thoughtfully. "Though our murderous baker had significantly more dramatic flair than our nervous pastry chef. Unless making perfect croissants is actually an elaborate cover for maritime crime."

"But if Alice was involved," I said slowly, "why would her parents be so protective? They seemed more worried about her than afraid for her."

Shawn returned from serving a group of newcomers, automatically wiping down the bar before rejoining our conversation. "Could be they don't know everything," he suggested. "Parents often don't."

The fireplace popped loudly, sending sparks dancing up the chimney. A gust of wind rattled the windows, making the hanging lamps sway slightly. Their movement cast shifting shadows across our small group, like nature itself was trying to add dramatic emphasis to our discussion.

"What we need," I said finally, "is to identify that woman from the rental shack. She took something – evidence, probably. Whatever Liam had found that made him both excited and nervous."

"The stars suggest-" Emma began, but was interrupted by a commotion near the door. A group of fishermen had just entered, stamping snow from their boots. Mike Sullivan was among them, his bandaged hand shoved deep in his pocket, his face set in grim lines. They chose a table far from the bar, but I noticed how their eyes swept the room before they settled.

"See what I mean?" Shawn murmured, nodding toward the newcomers. "They never used to be so cautious. Something's got them watching their backs."

"Or someone," Robert added quietly.

We sat in thoughtful silence for a moment, each processing the implications of everything we'd learned. The bar's warmth wrapped around us, creating a deceptive sense of security that contrasted sharply with the dangerous undercurrents we'd uncovered.

"Well," I said finally, pushing back from the bar. "I should head home. Need to clear my head, try to make sense of all this."

"Be careful, Jim," Emma said, her usual dreamy tone replaced by something more serious. "The stars suggest..."

she paused, rearranging her crystals one final time. "Just be careful."

"Always am," I assured her, though we all knew that wasn't entirely true.

"Thanks for the drinks, Shawn," I added, settling my bill. "And thanks, all of you, for the insights."

The walk home through the snow was quiet, the kind of stillness that only comes with fresh snowfall. Our footprints from earlier had already been filled in, erasing any evidence of our previous passage. The streetlights created pools of warm light in the darkness, each surrounded by a halo of falling snow.

"Quite a lot to process," Ginger observed as we walked, delicately picking his way through the snow. "The increasing complexity of this case makes our Christmas tree adventure seem almost straightforward in comparison."

"At least there were no riddles this time," I pointed out.

"No, just mysterious women with nautical tattoos, suspicious fishermen, and enough secrets to sink a fleet. Much simpler."

I chuckled despite the gravity of the situation. "When you put it that way..."

The snow continued to fall as we made our way home, adding another layer to the already white landscape. Somewhere in this quiet town, someone knew what had happened to Liam. Someone was watching, waiting, probably wondering how close we were getting to the truth.

"You know what bothers me most?" I said as we approached our house. "That woman from the rental shack – she knew exactly where to look. Like she'd been there before, knew what she was looking for."

"Indeed," Ginger agreed, shaking snow from his paws as we reached the porch. "Though I notice our list of suspects seems to grow with each conversation. Perhaps we should start a spreadsheet – though given your technological prowess, that might be overly optimistic."

The house was dark and quiet as we entered, but somehow comforting after the long day. I hung up my snow-dusted coat, my mind still turning over everything we'd learned. The mysterious woman from the rental shack seemed to be the key – find her, and we'd likely find the evidence Liam had gathered. Find the evidence, and we'd probably find his killer.

But as I prepared for bed, I couldn't shake the feeling that we were missing something obvious. Something that was right in front of us, if we could just see it clearly.

"Get some sleep, old man," Ginger advised, curling up in his favorite spot on the windowsill. "The mysteries of anchor tattoos and fishing quotas will still be there in the morning."

He was right, of course. Sleep would help clear my mind, maybe help me see the connections I was missing. Tomorrow we could start fresh, maybe talk to more people about that mysterious woman, try to identify her.

But as I drifted off to sleep, my dreams were filled with silhouettes on dark water, anchor tattoos that seemed to move of their own accord, and the endless sound of waves against the shore. Somewhere in this town, answers were waiting. We just had to figure out where to look.

# Chapter 13

The first rays of dawn had barely touched my bedroom window when my smartphone erupted in what sounded like a combination of whale songs, wind chimes, and what might have been Tibetan throat singing. Emma's latest contribution to my "spiritual awakening" via technology was apparently determined to start my day with cosmic chaos. The device vibrated across my nightstand with enough enthusiasm to suggest it was attempting to achieve lift-off.

"For the love of..." I fumbled for the phone, somehow managing to activate what sounded like rainfall on a tin roof, followed by what I strongly suspected was a recording of Emma herself chanting something about Mercury's position. My fingers, still clumsy with sleep, slid across the screen in increasingly desperate patterns.

"I see your morning battle with modern technology has begun early today," Ginger observed from his windowsill perch, where he'd been watching my struggles with evident amusement. "Though I must say, the combination of whale songs and your particular brand of morning coordination provides an interesting interpretive dance performance. Perhaps we should sell tickets."

The screen helpfully switched to what appeared to be a meditation timer, complete with soft bells and the soothing voice of someone explaining the importance of proper breathing techniques. In my attempts to silence it, I somehow managed to activate the Spanish language setting, resulting in the cosmic notifications now arriving in two languages.

"Right, cosmic alignment warnings sound significantly more dramatic in Spanish," Ginger commented, stretching languidly.

After what felt like hours but was probably only a few minutes, I finally managed to silence the celestial cacophony. The screen displayed a bewildering array of notifications: three different astrological alerts about Mercury's retrograde position, two meditation reminders, something about aligning my chakras, and – buried beneath all the cosmic clutter – an email from Dr. Chen sent at 3 AM.

The email stood out among Emma's spiritual spam like a lighthouse beam cutting through fog. Dr. Chen wanted to meet at noon in the town square. She had findings about Liam's death – findings that apparently couldn't wait for normal business hours.

"Dr. Chen wants to meet," I told Ginger, who had begun his morning grooming ritual with his usual methodical precision. Each stroke of his paw was carefully calculated, like a master artist at work. "Noon at the town square."

"Finally, our medical examiner emerges with actual scientific evidence," he commented between careful strokes. "How refreshing after our recent forays into celestial navigation and crystal-based investigation techniques."

The morning light strengthened as I made coffee, its rich aroma helping to ground me after the chaotic wake-up call. Outside, the fresh snow from last night sparkled like diamonds, unmarred except for a single set of paw prints that suggested Mr. Whiskers had already conducted his morning patrol of the neighborhood. The cardinal family that had claimed my bird feeder as their territory was already at work, their bright red plumage stark against the white landscape.

My kitchen, with its familiar worn counters and slightly temperamental stove, provided a comforting backdrop as I prepared breakfast. The morning sun caught the collection of coffee mugs on the shelf – each one telling its own story, from the chipped one Martha had given me years ago to the newer one Emma had presented me with, complete with zodiac symbols that supposedly enhanced the coffee's energy alignment.

"We have some time before meeting Dr. Chen," I said. "Maybe we should ask around about that mysterious woman with the anchor tattoo."

"Ah yes, our nautically-decorated friend from the rental shack," Ginger agreed, abandoning his grooming to join me at the breakfast table. The morning light caught his whiskers as he settled into his usual spot, making them gleam like fine silver threads. "Though given Robert's assessment of local tattoo prevalence, we might be searching for a very specific needle in a rather large maritime haystack."

The next few hours proved him right, turning into an exercise in small-town social dynamics that would have fascinated any anthropologist. Our first stop was the fish market, where Doris held court behind her counter like a queen on a throne of ice. Her white hair was tucked neatly under a hairnet, and her blue apron bore the stains of decades of expertise with seafood.

"Anchor tattoos?" she scoffed, her hands never stopping their practiced motion of filleting a cod. "Half the girls these days have them. It's all about that nautical aesthetic now. Though if you ask me, a real connection to the sea comes from gutting fish at five in the morning, not from pretty pictures on your ankle."

The morning crowd at Rose's café proved equally enlightening, if not particularly helpful. The breakfast rush was in full swing, the air thick with the mingled aromas of coffee, bacon, and Rose's famous seafood chowder. Every table seemed to have a theory about tattooed women in town, each more elaborate than the last.

"My niece has an anchor tattoo," old Chuck offered from his usual corner booth, his coffee cup leaving rings on the worn formica table. "But it's on her shoulder. Unless she's got another one I don't know about. Though these days, who knows what the young folks are up to?"

Even Mrs. Henderson, whose front porch served as an unofficial intelligence gathering station for town gossip, could only offer vague possibilities. Her rocking chair creaked rhythmically as she considered the question, her knitting needles clicking like miniature metronomes as she worked.

"There was a tourist last summer," she mused, her needles never slowing. "Had some kind of marking on her leg. Might have been an anchor, might have been a dolphin. Hard to tell with these modern designs. Though speaking of strange markings, did I tell you about my latest theory about the harbor seal population?"

\*\*\*

"I particularly enjoyed Mrs. Henderson's subsequent theory about the mysterious tattoo being a secret code for maritime smuggling operations," Ginger commented as we made our way through the snow-covered streets toward the town square. His paws left delicate impressions in the fresh snow, like an artist signing his work. "Though her suggestion that Mr. Whiskers might be involved in an underground catnip ring seems slightly far-fetched. That cat can barely organize his own grooming schedule, let alone a criminal enterprise."

The town square looked particularly picturesque in the winter sunlight, like something from a Christmas card that had somehow survived into January. The massive Christmas tree still stood in the center – a reminder of our holiday adventure with Everett, though it looked considerably less threatening now that it wasn't rigged with mechanical doom. Snow covered its branches, transforming last month's crime scene into something almost magical.

Small groups of people hurried across the square, their breath forming clouds in the cold air. The local coffee shop had set up a stand selling hot chocolate and cider, the steam rising from the cups creating temporary halos around their customers. A group of children were attempting to build a snowman near the benches, their laughter carrying across the square like music.

Dr. Chen arrived five minutes late, her practical boots leaving precise tracks in the snow that suggested both purpose and mild irritation. She wore a sensible dark coat that somehow managed to look both professional and slightly rebellious – much like the woman herself. Her black hair was pulled back in its usual no-nonsense style, though a few strands had escaped, suggesting a long night of work. Dark circles under her eyes hinted at hours spent in the morgue, though her gaze remained sharp and focused.

"Sorry I'm late," she said by way of greeting, adjusting her leather messenger bag with one gloved hand. "Had to dodge Miller in the parking lot. He was going on about tourist season impact statistics and 'community morale.'

That man would classify a meteor strike as a weather anomaly if it meant less paperwork."

We fell into step together, walking the perimeter of the square. The sound of our footsteps in the snow created an odd rhythm, punctuated by the distant calls of seagulls from the harbor and the cheerful shouts of children still attempting to perfect their snowman's rather lopsided appearance.

"I spent all night examining Liam's body," she continued, her voice low despite the relative privacy of our walk. The winter wind carried the scent of pine from the Christmas tree and something sweeter from the hot chocolate stand. "The findings are... interesting. And not at all supportive of Miller's convenient accident theory. That man wouldn't recognize evidence if it danced the macarena in his donut box."

"Our good doctor seems refreshingly direct," Ginger observed, delicately picking his way through the snow beside us. "Though I notice her opinion of Miller's investigative abilities aligns remarkably well with our own. Perhaps we should introduce her to Emma's crystal-based detection methods, just for variety."

"Tell me everything," I prompted, noting how Dr. Chen's hands were deep in her coat pockets, her shoulders tense with what seemed like frustrated professional pride. A woman used to being the smartest person in the room, forced to watch as her expertise was ignored in favor of expedience.

She paused our walk near a bench that someone had cleared of snow, though neither of us moved to sit. The cold air seemed to sharpen her words as she spoke. "I have two distinct theories about what happened that night."

Her dark eyes carried the intensity of someone who'd spent hours piecing together a puzzle that others were trying to ignore. She pulled a small notebook from her bag, flipping to a page covered in precise handwriting. "Primary theory: Liam got into a physical altercation on the dock. The bruises on his knuckles show he was fighting back – his right hand knuckles were particularly bruised, suggesting he landed at least one solid hit. During the struggle, he either fell or was pushed into the water. The head injury suggests he hit the boat or dock on the way down."

She turned a page, revealing detailed diagrams. "The toxicology results complicate things. Liam had alcohol in his system – not enough to be completely drunk, but enough to affect his coordination and judgment. That, combined with the freezing water temperature and the head injury..." She shook her head grimly. "Even a strong swimmer would have struggled."

"And Liam was an experienced swimmer," I noted, remembering Ms. Chambers' stories about his marine biology projects, his comfort on the water. A young man who'd spent countless hours studying tide pools and marine life, now a victim of the very environment he'd worked to protect.

"Which brings me to the alternative theory," Dr. Chen continued, tucking a stray strand of hair behind her ear with a gloved hand. "The alcohol suggests a different scenario. Someone could have taken advantage of his impaired state. They got him onto a boat – maybe to talk, maybe to confront him. The fight happened there, when he was already at a disadvantage. By the time he went into the water, he was already injured, disoriented from both the alcohol and likely a blow to the head. Whether he fell or was pushed at that point almost doesn't matter – he wouldn't have stood a chance."

The image of Mike Sullivan's bandaged hand flashed through my mind, though I kept that observation to myself for now. The winter sun had risen higher, making the snow almost blindingly bright. Children's laughter mixed with the calls of seagulls, creating a soundtrack that seemed inappropriately cheerful for our discussion of death at the docks.

"I've documented everything," Dr. Chen continued. "Photos, detailed notes, tissue samples – everything properly logged and filed. I even called in a favor from a colleague at the state lab for some specialized tests. Not that Miller's bothered to look at any of it." Her voice carried a bitter edge. "He's already writing up the accident report. Probably between donut runs."

She stopped again, turning to face me fully. The winter sun caught the determination in her eyes, the set of her jaw. A light dusting of snow had settled on her dark coat, creating a constellation of tiny crystals that sparkled as she moved. "Find out what really happened, Mr. Butterfield. Before Miller buries this case in bureaucratic convenience."

I shared what we'd learned – about the mysterious woman at the rental shack, about Danny Richards seeing two figures on a boat that night, about the growing tension among the local fishermen. Dr. Chen listened intently, occasionally nodding as pieces aligned with her physical evidence. Her gloved fingers moved across her notebook pages, making quick annotations as I spoke.

"The timing matches," she said, tapping her pen against a particular note. "Based on the examination of the body and other forensic evidence, I'd put time of death between 11 PM and 1 AM. Your witness's boat sighting fits right in that window." She frowned, adding another note. "And the presence of two people would explain some of the more unusual injury patterns."

"Whatever you're going to do," she said finally, checking her watch – a practical, no-nonsense timepiece that seemed to match its owner's personality, "do it soon. Miller wants this wrapped up by tomorrow. Says the town 'needs closure' before it affects the winter tourist season." Her tone suggested exactly what she thought of prioritizing tourism over truth.

\*\*\*

She left me standing in the snow-covered square, her precise footprints marking her path toward her car. The winter sun had reached its peak, making the fresh snow almost painfully bright. The children's snowman stood completed but slightly crooked, its coal eyes seeming to watch our parting with solemn interest.

I settled onto the bench, brushing away a light dusting of snow. Ginger hopped onto the back of the bench, arranging himself with his usual precise dignity. Just then, my phone buzzed with another notification. Not one of Emma's celestial alerts this time, but an email from an address I didn't recognize. The subject line made my breath catch: "Interesting night views from the docks."

"Either someone has developed a sudden passion for nocturnal maritime photography," Ginger observed, reading over my shoulder as I fumbled with the phone's screen settings, "or our mystery correspondent has decided to make things more interesting. Though I must say, their timing suggests a flair for the dramatic that rivals Emma's celestial predictions."

The message was brief but pointed: "Meet me at the docks at 9 PM alone (your cat doesn't count, you can bring him too)." The casual parenthetical about Ginger sent a chill down my spine that had nothing to do with the winter weather. Whoever this was, they'd been watching us closely enough to know about my feline partner.

An attachment icon blinked at me provocatively. After several fumbling attempts that somehow activated my phone's Spanish translation feature, turned on what sounded like a meditation gong, and briefly set my screen to what appeared to be "cosmic awareness mode" (another of Emma's helpful additions), I managed to open the video file.

The footage was dark and grainy, clearly taken from a distance, but I could make out Liam's rental boat bobbing near Robert's vessel. The running lights created a soft glow that illuminated two figures on board – a man and a woman, based on their silhouettes against the night sky. They appeared to be arguing, their gestures sharp and aggressive in the darkness. The woman's movements seemed familiar somehow, though the quality of the video and the distance made positive identification impossible. The clip lasted only five seconds before cutting off abruptly, like a door slamming on a conversation.

"Well," Ginger said after a moment of silence, "it seems our mystery correspondent has been holding onto some rather significant evidence. Though I notice they've mastered the art of dramatic timing. The theatrical pause before the big reveal – very film noir. All we're missing is the ominous background music and perhaps a fog machine."

I played the video again, trying to catch any detail I might have missed. The woman's movements, the way she gestured – something about it nagged at my memory, like a word on the tip of my tongue. The man's silhouette was larger, his stance aggressive. The boat bobbed gently in the dark water, its running lights transforming the ripples into shifting silver snakes.

The implications were clear – someone had witnessed what happened that night, someone who had chosen this moment to reach out. But why? And more importantly, who had been on that boat with Liam? The timing of this message, coming right after my conversation with Dr. Chen, seemed too perfect to be coincidental.

The winter sun continued its arc across the sky, the shadows in the square growing longer as afternoon approached. The snowman's coal eyes seemed to watch us with newfound interest, as if it too were trying to puzzle out the mystery. Somewhere in town, someone was waiting to see how I'd respond to their invitation. Someone who might have answers to questions that grew more complex with each new piece of information we uncovered.

"It seems," I said to Ginger, pocketing my phone, "we have plans for tonight."

"Indeed," he agreed, his tail swishing thoughtfully through the fresh snow. "Though I do hope our mysterious videographer has chosen a meeting spot with better protection from the elements than our last few adventures. My fur can only handle so much maritime drama. And given recent events, perhaps we should brush up on our swimming skills. Just in case."

The town square had begun to fill with its usual afternoon crowd – shoppers hurrying between errands, children released from school for lunch, the normal rhythm of small-town life continuing despite the secrets that seemed to lurk around every corner. Tonight, at the docks, someone was offering to share those secrets.

The question was: what price would they ask for their knowledge? And more importantly, could we trust someone who had waited until now to come forward?

# Chapter 14

I sat on the bench where Dr. Chen had delivered her unsettling findings, Ginger still perched beside me, the mysterious email's implications weighing heavily on my mind. My phone felt unusually heavy in my pocket, as if the video file it contained had actual physical mass. Nine o'clock seemed impossibly far away, each tick of the town hall clock marking time with maddening slowness.

"You know," I said to Ginger, who was still meticulously grooming snow from his paws with the focused dedication of an artist restoring a masterpiece, "waiting around for someone else's revelation seems like a waste of time. Especially when we might be able to piece this together ourselves."

"Ah yes," Ginger replied, pausing his grooming to fix me with his characteristic blend of amusement and skepticism. "Confronting potential murderers is such a sensible alternative to patience. Though I suppose it would save us the trouble of standing around in the cold later. And your track record with confrontations has been so stellar lately."

The last few children were gathering their belongings, reluctantly abandoning their crooked snowman to whatever fate awaited it. A mother called out reminders about mittens and homework, her voice carrying that particular tone of resigned authority unique to parents of winter-loving kids.

"Think about it," I pressed, watching as one small boy made a final adjustment to the snowman's carrot nose, which already listed decidedly to the left. "Mike Sullivan's bandaged hand, that mysterious woman at Liam's shack, the two figures Danny Richards saw on the boat – it can't all be coincidence. The pieces are there, we just need to make them fit."

"And your proposed solution is to what? March up to our temperamental fisherman and demand explanations?" Ginger's tail twitched with a mixture of amusement and concern, sending small puffs of snow flying from where he sat. "I'm sure that will go splendidly. Perhaps we should write our wills first, just to be efficient. Though I must say, death by angry fisherman would make for an interesting obituary."

A gust of wind swept across the square, carrying the mixed scents of pine from the Christmas tree, sugary sweetness from the hot chocolate stand, and something savory that could only be coming from Rose's café. The aroma triggered a memory – Mike Sullivan's predictable habits, his daily routines that were as regular as the tides themselves.

"Rose's," I said decisively, already turning toward the café. "Mike and his crew always have lunch there around this time. We can talk to them in public, where they're less likely to do anything... dramatic."

"Right, public locations have worked so well in preventing violence in this town," Ginger muttered, but he was already moving alongside me, his paws leaving precise impressions in the fresh snow. "Though being thrown through a window at Rose's would at least come with the consolation of excellent chowder. And possibly a front-row seat to whatever maritime justice Miller would bumble through."

\*\*\*

The café's windows glowed invitingly against the winter afternoon, steam fogging the glass where it met the cold air outside. Through the clouded panes, I could make out the usual lunchtime crowd – fishermen warming up between trips to their boats, locals seeking refuge from the cold, the regulars who treated Rose's counter like their personal office space.

The bell above the door announced our arrival with its familiar chime, releasing a wave of warmth scented with coffee, fried fish, and Rose's signature chowder. The floorboards, worn smooth by generations of salt-crusted boots, creaked softly under my feet. The ancient ceiling fans spun lazily overhead, their blades collecting decades of stories along with a fine patina of cooking oil and sea spray.

But Mike's usual corner booth – the one with the best view of both the harbor and the door – sat conspicuously empty.

Rose looked up from where she was refilling coffee cups, her lined face creasing into a welcoming smile that didn't quite reach her eyes. Her white apron remained mysteriously spotless despite the lunch rush, and her silver hair was tucked neatly under the same hairnet she'd worn yesterday. "Jim! And Ginger too. Your usual?"

"Actually, I was looking for Mike Sullivan," I said, scanning the lunch crowd more thoroughly.

"Ah," Rose's smile faltered slightly, her hands automatically wiping down an already clean section of counter. "His boys came in earlier. When I asked about Mike, they said he was eating at home today." She straightened a stack of menus that needed no straightening, a gesture that seemed more nervous than practical. "Bit odd, that."

"Odd how?"

"Well, Mike's been coming here for lunch every day for fifteen years – unless he's out at sea, of course. Man's got his routines, you know? More regular than the tide charts. Can't remember the last time he ate at home during work hours."

The café's usual lunchtime buzz continued around us – the clink of spoons against bowls, the hiss of the ancient coffee maker, the steady thrum of conversations pitched just low enough to maintain the illusion of privacy. But something felt off, like a familiar song played slightly out of tune.

"Would you happen to have his address?" I asked, trying to sound casual while watching Rose's reaction. "There are some things I'd like to discuss with him."

Rose hesitated, her hand hovering over her order pad. Finally, she pulled out the pad and began writing. "It's over on Maple Street – the blue house with the white trim, can't miss it. Though Jim?" She paused, her face serious. "Be careful. Mike's been… different lately. More on edge, if you take my meaning."

"Our good Rose has mastered the art of understating potential danger," Ginger commented as we left the café, the bell's cheerful goodbye seeming somehow ominous. "Though she didn't mention whether Mike's new edge might involve a propensity for disposing of nosy investigators in the harbor. Perhaps we should have asked about his preferred method of dealing with unwanted visitors."

*** 

The walk to Maple Street took us through the older part of town, where generations of sea captains and fishermen had built homes with wide porches and widow's walks – architectural remnants of days when wives would watch for returning ships. The houses here had character that newer construction couldn't match, each one weathered by decades of salt air and storms but maintained with the particular pride that seemed unique to coastal communities.

The winter afternoon light caught the ice formations hanging from the eaves, transforming them into crystal sculptures that would have delighted Emma's mystical sensibilities. Here and there, someone had hung wind chimes that tinkled softly in the sea breeze, their music mixing with the distant sound of waves.

Mike's house stood out even among its well-kept neighbors. The blue paint looked fresh, almost defiantly so against the winter sky, while the white trim remained crisp enough to suggest recent attention. Fishing nets hung decoratively along the porch rails, though their worn condition and subtle mending indicated they'd seen actual use rather than being mere maritime decoration. A collection of buoys adorned one wall, their faded colors telling stories of years at sea. The brass door knocker had been polished to a shine that caught the afternoon sun like a winking eye.

"Well," Ginger observed as we approached the front steps, his tail held low in what I recognized as his investigative posture, "at least if this is indeed a killer's den, it's a very well-maintained one. Though I notice a distinct lack of emergency exits. And that garden gnome by the steps seems suspiciously judgmental."

The porch boards creaked softly under my feet – solid oak, worn smooth by years of use but still sturdy. A pair of fishing boots stood neatly by the door, caked with what looked like fresh harbor mud. The welcome mat bore an intricate compass rose design, though the 'welcome' part seemed somewhat ironic given our purpose.

Before I could reach for the knocker, the door opened to reveal a woman about Mike's age, her brown hair pulled back in a practical bun that somehow managed to look both severe and elegant. She wore a cable-knit sweater that looked hand-made, its intricate patterns suggesting hours of patient work. Her eyes – sharp and assessing despite her pleasant expression – reminded me of harbor birds watching for fish just beneath the surface.

"Can I help you?" Her voice carried the slight roughness common to longtime coastal residents, though her tone remained carefully polite. A faint aroma of something cooking drifted from behind her – garlic and herbs, mixed with the unmistakable scent of fresh-caught fish.

"I'm looking for Mike," I said, noting how her fingers tightened slightly on the doorframe at the mention of his name. "I'm Jim Butterfield. I'd like to talk to him about some recent events in town."

Something flickered behind her eyes – concern? fear? – but her smile never wavered, like a skilled actor hitting their mark. "Ah, the private investigator. Mike's mentioned you." Her gaze flicked past me briefly, scanning the street before she opened the door wider. "I'm Patricia, Mike's wife. He's home – why don't you join us for lunch? I just finished cooking."

Her gaze dropped to Ginger, and her smile became more genuine, softening the sharp edges of her previous expression. "Your cat is welcome too. I'm sure I can find something suitable in the kitchen. We always have fresh fish."

"Suitable?" Ginger muttered as we followed Patricia inside, his whiskers twitching with barely contained skepticism. "I do hope her definition of suitable extends beyond fish heads and sympathy."

The house's interior carried the competing scents of lemon polish and whatever was cooking – fish stew, maybe, rich with herbs and garlic that spoke of old family recipes passed down through generations. Family photos lined the walls in neat chronological order, showing Mike and Patricia through the years, often on boats or at the harbor. Their children's growth could be tracked through school pictures and fishing trips, a visual timeline of a life built around the sea. A family Bible held a place of honor on a side table, its well-worn cover suggesting regular use.

Patricia led us to a spacious kitchen where sunlight streamed through windows that offered a view of the harbor in the distance, the water glinting like scattered diamonds in the winter light. The room was spotless, everything arranged with the precision of someone who valued order above all else. Copper pots hung in gleaming rows, and herbs dried in neat bundles from ceiling hooks. A pot simmered on the stove, steam rising to fog the windows.

"Mike!" Patricia called up the stairs, her voice carrying that particular pitch wives develop after years of summoning husbands to meals. "Lunch is ready, and we have guests!"

Heavy footsteps descended the stairs – deliberate, measured, like someone trying very hard to appear casual. Mike's bulk filled the kitchen doorway, his presence seeming to make the spacious room suddenly smaller. His bandaged hand was shoved deep in his pocket, and tension radiated from his shoulders despite his attempt at a relaxed stance. I noticed his other hand stayed close to the counter, near where a set of kitchen knives hung on a magnetic strip.

"Jim," he said, his voice carefully neutral though his eyes were anything but. "What brings you to my home?"

"I just have some follow-up questions from our conversation yesterday," I replied, matching his tone while noting how he positioned himself between Patricia and me. "Your wife kindly invited us to join you for lunch."

"Did she now?" Something passed between husband and wife – a look that carried whole conversations in its brevity, the kind of silent communication that comes from decades of marriage. Then Mike's shoulders relaxed slightly, though his bandaged hand remained hidden. "Well, can't turn down Patricia's cooking. Have a seat."

The kitchen chairs scraped softly against the well-worn floor as we settled around the table. A delicate china bowl decorated with sailing ships served as a centerpiece, filled with seashells collected from who knew how many beach walks. The afternoon light caught the worn spots on the table's surface, telling stories of countless family meals and morning coffees.

Patricia moved through the kitchen with practiced efficiency, her movements suggesting years of orchestrating meals around fishing schedules and tide charts. She first set down a small plate of what looked like premium salmon for Ginger, the fish arranged with the kind of care usually reserved for fine dining establishments.

"I save the best parts," she explained, her smile genuine as she watched Ginger examine the offering. "We used to have cats when we first moved to this house – they're particular about their fish. This one's fresh from this morning's catch."

"Finally, someone who understands proper feline dining standards," Ginger commented, though I noticed he waited for Patricia to turn away before sampling the salmon. His whiskers twitched appreciatively despite his attempt at suspicion. "Though I maintain a healthy skepticism about accepting food in potential suspects' homes. Even if it is perfectly seared."

The kitchen filled with the gentle sounds of Patricia's cooking routine – the soft clink of spoons against bowls, the whisper of her apron as she moved between stove and table, the quiet confidence of someone completely in their element. She served the rest of us generous bowls of fish stew, steam rose from the bowls in delicate spirals.

The walls here bore more family photos – graduation ceremonies, wedding days, first fishing trips. One showed a younger Mike and Patricia on what must have been their first boat, both grinning into the camera with the particular joy of people at the beginning of a shared adventure. It struck me how that same boat appeared in later photos, clearly maintained with care over the years until it was finally replaced by the larger commercial vessel Mike now captained.

Mike watched me studying the photos, his expression unreadable. The bandage on his hand had been changed recently – the gauze looked fresh, though a small spot of red had already begun to seep through. His wedding ring bulged slightly beneath the wrapping, suggesting he'd refused to remove it even for treatment.

"The stew is my grandmother's recipe," Patricia said, perhaps sensing the growing tension. She reached toward a high shelf, stretching for what appeared to be an old copper pepper mill. "She always said a proper fish stew needs fresh-ground pepper, not that store-bought powder."

As she stretched upward, her movements caused her pant leg to ride up slightly at the ankle. Ginger's paw suddenly pressed against my leg, his claws extending just enough to get my attention without being obvious.

"Jim," he hissed urgently, his voice barely a whisper. "Her ankle – look!"

I glanced down as casually as I could, trying to maintain the pretense of a friendly lunch visit, and felt my breath catch. There, just visible above her left sock, was an anchor tattoo – not just similar to the one Ginger had described seeing on the mysterious woman at the rental shack, but identical. A small, professionally done piece that matched Ginger's description perfectly.

The revelation hit me like a physical blow. Patricia Sullivan – respected fisherman's wife, skilled cook, seemingly perfect hostess – had been the woman in the shack. Which meant she'd also likely been the figure in the video, arguing with Liam on his boat in the darkness before his death.

The pepper mill clinked softly as Patricia set it on the table, the sound somehow ominous in the suddenly charged atmosphere of the sunny kitchen. She smoothed her pant leg in what might have been a casual gesture but felt deliberate, like closing a door that had been accidentally left open.

Mike's eyes hadn't missed my glance at his wife's ankle. His bandaged hand shifted on the table, the movement emphasizing rather than concealing its injury. The message was clear – he knew that I knew, and now we had to decide what to do about it.

We sat frozen in this moment of mutual recognition, like players in a game where the next move could change everything.

The question was: who would make that move first?

# Chapter 15

The kitchen's warmth suddenly felt stifling, the rich aroma of fish stew cloying rather than inviting. Patricia's hands remained steady as she set out thick slices of homemade bread beside each bowl. The bread looked fresh-baked, probably from that morning.

I glanced at Mike's bandaged hand resting on the table, then back at Patricia's ankle where that telling tattoo had revealed itself.

"I've been hearing some interesting rumors lately," I said carefully, breaking the charged silence. "About fishing quotas being exceeded. Any truth to that?"

Mike's face remained impressively neutral, though his fingers twitched slightly against the tablecloth's faded pattern of anchors and compass roses. "Rumors are like seagulls in this town," he replied, his voice steady. "Always circling, making noise, but usually just fighting over scraps of nothing."

The homey setting made what I had to say next feel almost sacrilegious, like breaking bad news in a church. But we were past the point of polite evasion. The afternoon light had begun to fade, casting longer shadows across the kitchen floor.

"Then perhaps you can explain," I said, watching their faces carefully, "why someone who looks remarkably like your wife, with an identical anchor tattoo, was seen taking something from Liam's rental shack during yesterday's protest?"

The effect was immediate. Patricia's spoon clattered against her bowl, sending tiny droplets of stew onto the pristine tablecloth – small dark spots that spread like secrets finally coming to light. Mike's bandaged hand clenched into a fist, then relaxed with visible effort. They exchanged a look that carried years of shared secrets and silent communication, the kind of understanding that only comes from weathering life's storms together.

"It's all your fault," Patricia murmured to Mike, her voice barely above a whisper but carrying clearly in the suddenly silent kitchen. "I had to clean up your mess. Again." Her hands smoothed her apron – a nervous gesture that seemed at odds with her earlier confidence.

She turned to me, her earlier hostess warmth replaced by something harder, more resigned. The afternoon light caught the silver strands in her hair, making them shine like threads of steel. "What exactly did you see?"

"Just what I said – a woman taking something from a dead man's shack." I kept my voice level, though my heart was racing. Beside me, I could feel Ginger's muscles tensing, ready for whatever might come next. His tail had stopped its usual lazy swish, now held perfectly still – his version of high alert.

"You might want to consider your next words carefully," Ginger murmured, his eyes fixed on Mike's bandaged hand. "Though I must say, the salmon suggests a certain culinary expertise that would be a shame to waste on prison food."

But instead of the explosion I'd half-expected, both Mike and Patricia seemed to deflate slightly, like sails when the wind dies. The kitchen felt smaller somehow, more intimate, as if the walls themselves were leaning in to hear what would come next.

"Yes," Patricia said finally, her fingers tracing the pattern on her teacup. "It was-"

"Let me tell it," Mike interrupted, placing his bandaged hand over his wife's. The gesture was gentle, protective – a sharp contrast to the angry man I'd seen at the Salty Breeze. "It's my mess, like you said." He looked at me directly, his weathered face showing a mix of resignation and relief. "No point in holding back now. You're like a dog with a bone when you get onto something – saw that during your previous cases."

"And there's no evidence left anyway," Patricia added softly, her gaze drifting to a drawer near the sink.

"Evidence?" I asked, noting how the word seemed to catch in the air between us.

Mike shifted in his chair, the wood creaking softly beneath his bulk. The fading daylight caught the silver in his beard, making him look older somehow, more vulnerable than the aggressive fisherman I'd encountered at the Salty Breeze.

"Let me start from the beginning," he said, absently adjusting the bandage that wrapped his right hand. A small spot of red had begun to seep through the white gauze, like a warning flag. "First off – neither of us killed Liam. I know what you're thinking, looking at my hand, putting pieces together. But killing? That's forbidden waters for us."

He glanced around his kitchen, at the family photos lining the walls, the children's art projects proudly displayed on the refrigerator – crayon drawings of boats and fish, school certificates, a recent report card covered in A's. "We've got kids at school right now, thank God not hearing this conversation. I'm not saying I'm a saint – sure, I've thrown punches when pushed, lost my temper more than I should. But murder?" He shook his head firmly, the gesture carrying the weight of absolute certainty.

Patricia stood, moving to the stove with the mechanical precision of someone needing to keep their hands busy. The soft clink of her wooden spoon against the pot provided a gentle counterpoint to Mike's rough voice. Steam rose from the stew, fogging the window behind her where the harbor lights had begun to twinkle in the gathering dusk.

"It started a few months back," Mike continued, his eyes fixed on his bandaged hand. His weathered fingers traced the edge of the gauze, as if trying to find the beginning of a story wound too tightly to easily unravel. "This contractor from a fishing factory in the city came around. Had what he called a 'lucrative opportunity' – fancy words for breaking the law, but he made it sound so reasonable. Double our usual catch, look the other way on quotas, make some extra money on the side."

The kitchen had grown darker as he spoke, shadows gathering in the corners like waiting audiences. A gust of wind rattled the windowpanes, carrying with it the sharp scent of approaching snow.

"The timing seemed like a gift," Patricia added softly, still stirring the stew that no one was eating anymore. "With college coming up for the kids, prices rising everywhere... You should see the tuition bills nowadays." She gestured toward a stack of papers on the counter, their official letterheads visible even in the fading light.

"Our very own dilemma of maritime morality," Ginger observed quietly, having finished his salmon but remaining alertly focused on the unfolding conversation. "Though I notice ethical flexibility seems to increase proportionally with profit margins. Rather like my own standards for acceptable fish preparation."

"So we took the deal," Mike admitted, reaching for his coffee mug but not drinking from it. The ceramic seemed to ground him somehow, giving his restless hands something to hold onto. "Started catching double, fudging the paperwork. It was easy – too easy, really. Should've known better." He laughed without humor, the sound hollow in the dimming kitchen. "But Liam... somehow that kid got a hold of our paperwork. The monthly reports we sent to the factory, documentation of the real catches versus what we reported officially."

Patricia moved to turn on the lights, but Mike's voice stopped her. "Leave them," he said softly. The growing darkness seemed to make confession easier, as if some truths were too harsh for full illumination. The only light now came from the harbor through the windows and the soft glow above the stove, casting everyone in shades of blue and amber.

"Two days ago, Liam cornered me by my boat," Mike continued, his voice dropping lower. "Started talking about evidence, about exposing everything. He was fired up, passionate – you know how he could get when he thought he was fighting for something right." His voice caught slightly on the word 'right', as if the concept itself had become complicated. "I panicked. Did something stupid."

"Stupider than exceeding fishing quotas?" I prompted gently. In the dimness, I could just make out the family photos on the walls, their happy faces seeming to watch our conversation with increasing concern.

Mike's laugh was harsh in the gathering darkness. "Yeah. Much stupider. That night – Liam's last night – I went to his rental shack. It was dark, thought I'd break in, find whatever evidence he had before he could use it."

The wall clock ticked steadily in the background, marking time as Mike's story unfolded. Outside, the first snowflakes had begun to fall, visible in the cone of light from the porch lamp.

"The plan seemed simple enough when I first thought of it," Mike continued, his eyes distant as if watching the scene replay itself. "Get in, find the papers, get out. But you know what they say about plans." He traced a pattern on the tablecloth with his uninjured hand, following the faded anchor design. "The lock was stubborn – took more force than I expected. That's how I really messed up my hand, not from some fight like everyone probably thought."

Patricia had stopped pretending to cook now, standing motionless by the stove as her husband spoke. The only movement in the kitchen was the gentle sway of dried herbs hanging from their hooks, stirred by the heat from the vent, and the steady fall of snow visible through the windows.

"I stepped inside," Mike went on, his voice dropping even lower. "Dark as a storm at midnight in there, could barely see anything. But the smell – alcohol fumes strong enough to make your eyes water. And there was Liam, slumped over his desk like he'd just dropped where he sat."

"Then I made another mistake," Mike said, running his good hand through his graying hair. "Stepped on this old floorboard – the kind that's been waiting years to betray someone. Made a sound like a gunshot in that quiet." He shook his head, remembering. "Liam came up from that desk like a hooked marlin. Threw a punch that would've taken my head off if he'd been steadier on his feet. Hit the wall instead – probably explains the bruises on his knuckles that doctor found."

The kitchen had grown so dark now that faces were mostly shadows, features suggested rather than revealed. The harbor lights through the window painted everything in shifting patterns of gold and shadow, like an old film playing out in real time.

"For a second there," Mike's voice had dropped to barely above a whisper, "I thought about taking advantage of his state. He was drunk, unsteady. One good push would've put him down long enough to find those papers. It would've been easy." He looked up, meeting my eyes squarely despite the dim light. "But I couldn't do it. Sure, we've had our fights at the Salty Breeze, but that's different – he'd be ready, on equal ground. But taking advantage of someone in that state? That's not the kind of man I am."

Patricia had moved back to the table, placing her hand on Mike's shoulder. The gesture carried years of shared struggles and support, speaking louder than any words could have.

"So I ran," Mike said simply. "Could hear him behind me, cursing up a storm, probably taking out his frustration on the walls." He flexed his bandaged hand again. "Next morning..."

The silence that followed was heavy with unspoken weight. Even the wall clock seemed to tick more softly, as if reluctant to intrude on the moment.

"Next morning we heard about Liam," Patricia picked up the thread when Mike's voice failed him. She switched on a small lamp near the sink, its warm glow creating a gentle circle of light that seemed to hold us all in its confession. "Mike told me about the papers still in the shack. Papers that could ruin everything – our business, our family's future." Her voice hardened slightly, taking on an edge like winter waves against the shore. "So yes, I went in during the protest. Used the chaos as cover. Got the evidence."

The snow was falling more heavily now, visible through the kitchen windows as a white curtain against the darkness. The harbor lights had become soft glows in the distance, like stars fallen to earth. Each snowflake caught the light as it passed, creating an ever-changing display that seemed oddly beautiful against the gravity of our conversation.

"Where are they now?" I asked, watching their faces carefully in the lamp's gentle illumination.

Patricia moved to a drawer without hesitation, her steps sure despite the dim light. She pulled out a manila envelope, worn at the edges as if it had been handled many times, along with another document that looked newer, more official.

"The papers are here," she said, placing them on the table between us. The envelope made a soft scratching sound against the tablecloth. "Along with this – notice of contract termination with the fishing factory. Signed this morning."

"The final act of maritime redemption," Ginger commented softly, his eyes reflecting the lamp light as he watched the scene unfold. "Though I notice timing often improves remarkably when evidence becomes inconvenient."

I examined both documents carefully while Mike continued speaking. His voice had taken on a different quality now – less defensive, more resigned, like someone who'd finally put down a heavy burden they'd been carrying for too long.

"We have no idea what really happened to Liam that night," he said, absently rubbing his bandaged hand. The gauze was definitely showing more spots of red now, but he seemed beyond noticing. "Maybe he got drunker, fell in. But it wasn't us." His voice carried a weight of sincerity that was hard to discount. "We made mistakes, broke laws we shouldn't have. But murder? No."

The truth of their story settled around us like the snow outside – layer upon layer building up to something undeniable. Their actions made sense – the kind of sense that comes from desperation and opportunity rather than malice. If Mike had killed Liam that night, he could have easily taken the papers then. Patricia's later risk would have been unnecessary. The pieces didn't fit for the Sullivans to be killers, even if they were guilty of other crimes.

Looking around their kitchen in the soft lamplight – at the family photos spanning decades on the walls, the children's artwork proudly displayed, the well-worn comfort of a home filled with love despite its imperfections – I knew they were telling the truth. Their crime was exceeding fishing quotas, not murder. Even the china cabinet in the corner spoke of stability, of lives built carefully over years, its shelves lined with wedding gifts and inherited pieces that had survived countless family gatherings.

"Dylan and his environmental group will be watching your crew more closely now," I said finally, standing. The chair scraped softly against the floor – a homey sound that seemed to break the spell of confession. "Especially after what happened to Liam."

Mike nodded grimly, his face catching the mixed light from the lamp and the snow-reflected harbor glow outside. "Let them. We've got nothing to hide anymore. Made our choice this morning when we ended that contract." He glanced at a photo of his children on the wall – a recent school picture showing bright, hopeful faces. "Maybe it's better this way. Teaching them about doing what's right, even when it's hard."

"Jim," he said suddenly, his voice tight with worry. "I know I made a mistake, but if word about the quotas gets out..." He glanced at the family photos again, his weathered face showing real fear. "My career would be over. I wouldn't be able to provide for my family anymore."

"Your secret's safe with me," I assured him, understanding the weight of what I was promising. "As long as you keep your word about ending it. No more deals like this."

"Never again," he said firmly, the relief evident in his voice. "We'll do things right from now on."

Patricia walked us to the door, her earlier hostess warmth replaced by something more genuine – the relief of someone who's finally put down a heavy burden. The porch light came on automatically as we stepped outside, creating a pool of warm light in the gathering dusk. The snow had transformed their front yard into something from a winter postcard, unmarked except for our earlier footprints, now slowly filling in.

"Be careful, Mr. Butterfield," she said softly as we left. "Whoever really killed Liam… they're still out there." Her voice carried both warning and gratitude – a complex mixture that seemed to sum up our entire evening.

The evening had turned significantly colder during our visit, the wind carrying a sharp bite that hadn't been there earlier. Stars were beginning to appear in breaks between the snow clouds, their light competing with the street lamps that had flickered to life while we were inside.

"Well," Ginger said as we walked away from the Sullivan house, his paws leaving delicate prints in the fresh snow, "that was certainly more dramatic than our usual lunch invitations. Though I must say, the salmon was excellent. Even if it was technically obtained through questionable quota practices."

I checked my watch in the glow of a street lamp – still several hours until our mysterious meeting at the docks. At least we'd ruled out two suspects, even if we'd uncovered a different kind of crime in the process. But the identity of the woman on that boat with Liam remained unclear, a shadow still waiting to be brought into the light. Soon, we might finally learn who that was.

"Well, we have hours until our cryptic correspondent's dramatic reveal," Ginger said, his tail held high despite the falling snow. "Plenty of time for a proper meal that doesn't involve questioning potential suspects. Though I notice that does seem to be becoming our standard dining routine."

He had a point. We'd learned a lot today – maybe too much. Some time to process everything would help. And food that didn't come with a side of confession might be a nice change of pace.

In a few hours, we'd meet our mysterious correspondent at the docks. Maybe then we'd finally get the answers we needed. Or maybe we'd just find more questions – it seemed to be the pattern lately.

Either way, we'd be ready. We had to be. For Liam's sake, and for the truth that someone in this town was trying very hard to keep hidden beneath the falling snow.

# Chapter 16

The docks at night carried a different kind of silence than during the day – not the absence of sound, but rather a collection of softer noises that seemed to belong specifically to the darkness. Waves lapped gently against weathered pilings, rigging clinked softly against masts, and somewhere in the distance, a foghorn mourned across the dark water. The winter night air carried a sharp bite that made every breath feel crystalline, while the lights from the moored boats created shifting patterns on the black water like fallen stars.

The snow had stopped falling, but a thick blanket of white covered the docks, unmarked except for our footprints and what looked like raccoon tracks leading to an overturned trash bin. Mist rose from the harbor in delicate wisps, creating an otherworldly atmosphere that seemed appropriate for clandestine meetings.

"Well," Ginger observed as we approached our designated meeting spot, his paws leaving precise impressions in the pristine snow, "at least our mysterious correspondent chose a scenic location for potential malfeasance. Though

I notice a distinct lack of emergency exits. Unless you've suddenly developed an aptitude for swimming in freezing water."

The bench where we'd been instructed to wait sat at the edge of the dock, its wooden slats frosted with snow and its metal arms gleaming dully in the scattered light from nearby boats. Behind it, Robert's boat creaked gently at its mooring, its dark bulk a reminder of recent tragedy.

"Ah," a familiar voice called from the shadows. "Right on time."

The journalist from the B&B stepped into the light, and somehow I wasn't surprised. He'd shed his expensive wool coat for something darker and more practical, though his designer glasses still caught the light when he moved. A leather messenger bag hung at his side, its contents clearly precious based on how carefully he held it.

"You know, watching you and your remarkable cat play detective these past few days has been quite entertaining," the journalist said, brushing snow from the bench before sitting. His movements were deliberate, practiced – the gestures of someone used to controlling situations.

The way he said "remarkable cat" made my skin crawl slightly. He gestured to the space beside him on the bench, his smile never reaching his eyes. "Please, sit. I have something to show you."

The wood was cold through my coat as I sat, maintaining a careful distance. Up close, I could smell expensive cologne – something trying too hard to be sophisticated

– and what might have been scotch on his breath. His messenger bag made a soft sound as he opened it, leather against leather, and withdrew what looked like a tablet in a waterproof case.

"I suppose I should introduce myself properly," he said, his fingers moving across the tablet's screen with practiced efficiency. His manicured nails caught the light from a nearby boat, each one perfectly shaped and buffed. "Thomas Reid, freelance journalist. Though lately I've been focusing on more... specialized stories."

"You mean blackmail," I said flatly.

He laughed, the sound carrying none of the warmth it pretended to. "Such an ugly word. I prefer to think of it as negotiated truth management." The tablet's screen cast a blue glow across his features, making them seem somehow harder. "But before we discuss terms, I believe you'll want to see this."

Thomas leaned forward as he started the video, his body language betraying an unsettling eagerness. His fingers tapped against the tablet's case in an irregular rhythm, like a conductor directing a particularly dark symphony. The expensive watch on his wrist – probably worth more than most fishermen made in a month – caught the dim light with each movement.

The video started without preamble – clearly shot from some distance. Liam's rental boat approached Robert's vessel, its running lights creating a soft glow that illuminated two figures on deck. Their voices carried across the water, distorted by distance but growing clearer as the boat drew nearer.

"Watch carefully now," Thomas murmured, his voice carrying the same anticipatory tension I'd heard in documentary narrators just before the predator strikes. "This is where it gets... interesting."

The way he savored that last word sent a chill through me. Every few seconds, his eyes would dart from the tablet's screen to study my reaction, his expression reminiscent of a food critic sampling an exotic dish – analytical, detached, yet somehow hungry.

On screen, Liam's movements were erratic, uncoordinated. His gestures became increasingly aggressive as he advanced toward the woman on the boat. Even through the grainy footage, his intoxication was evident in every stumbling step. The woman backed away, her movements careful, controlled – someone used to maintaining balance on a moving deck.

The confrontation escalated quickly. Liam lunged forward, his movements clumsy but forceful. The woman – her face still unclear in the darkness – sidestepped with the fluid grace of someone who'd spent considerable time on boats. As Liam's momentum carried him past her, she used his own force against him, a defensive move that spoke of instinct rather than aggression.

Distant, indistinct sounds of their conflict carried across the water – sharp cries and the hollow thump of feet on the deck. Liam recovered, turning to make another grab.

This time, the woman deflected his arms, pushing them wide rather than engaging directly. Her every move was defensive, focused on creating distance rather than causing harm.

The fatal moment unfolded with horrible clarity. Liam, frustrated by his failed attempts, charged forward again. But the woman twisted away from his grasp. And Liam's momentum, unchecked by contact and amplified by his intoxication, carried him straight to the boat's edge. For a terrible second, he teetered there, arms windmilling against the night sky.

Then he fell.

The sound of his head hitting Robert's boat was distinct even through the tablet's speakers. From the boat, a woman's voice – high with panic and horror – called out into the darkness. The camera caught her rushing to the rail, her movements frantic now as she searched the water's surface. Nothing but gentle waves answered her increasingly desperate calls.

As Liam's body disappeared beneath the dark water, the woman's desperate movements became more frantic. The camera caught her leaning over the rail, her voice carrying across the water in increasingly panicked cries. Her silhouette moved back and forth along the deck, checking different angles, clearly hoping Liam would surface.

The woman managed to dock the boat with shaking hands, her movements automatic despite her obvious distress. As she fled past the camera's position, her face caught the light briefly – young, terrified, and unmistakably Alice's.

Thomas's smile grew wider as the video ended, his expression carrying the satisfied look of someone who'd played this moment many times in private, studying it, savoring it, planning how best to use it. His designer glasses reflected the tablet's glow, turning his eyes into blank blue screens that revealed nothing while seeing everything.

He sat back, adjusting his position on the bench with theatrical precision. Everything about him seemed calculated – from the casual way he held the tablet just out of reach, to the practiced tilt of his head that showed off his expensive haircut to best advantage.

"You know," he said, producing a monogrammed handkerchief to clean his glasses, "in my line of work, timing is everything. When to reveal, when to withhold, when to… negotiate." He replaced his glasses with the same care someone else might handle a loaded weapon. "Rather like chess, wouldn't you say?"

"It was an accident," I said quietly, the pieces finally falling into place. "She was defending herself. He was drunk, aggressive – she didn't push him."

"Details, details," Thomas waved his hand dismissively, though his eyes remained sharp behind his expensive frames. "The public rarely cares about such nuances. They'll see what they want to see – a confrontation, a death, a woman fleeing the scene. The internet especially loves that kind of ambiguity. Gives everyone something to argue about in the comments section."

"So that's your game," I said, watching how his fingers kept touching the tablet protectively, like a miser with his gold. "Blackmail. Show me the video, then use me to pressure Alice's family for money." It was a scenario I'd read about in dozens of crime novels – the intermediary approach, using someone trusted by the target to make the demands. Classic technique, if not particularly creative.

His smile widened slightly, showing too many teeth. "Smart man. You see, I've grown rather tired of watching you and your remarkable feline friend running around town, asking questions, stirring things up. Much simpler to show you the truth and let you be my... intermediary."

I found myself eyeing the tablet in Thomas's hands, calculating the odds. Despite my age, with Ginger's help, we could probably snatch it before he could react. But the thought was pointless – someone this calculating would certainly have backup copies stored somewhere safe. Besides, stealing evidence would only complicate an already messy situation.

"You have twenty-four hours," Thomas said, checking his watch. "Return here tomorrow night, same time, with a bag containing fifty thousand dollars. Cash only, naturally."

"Or what? You'll release the video?" The night air carried the sharp scent of approaching snow, mixing with the ever-present brine of the harbor. "Show everyone what really happened? That it was an accident?"

"I'll show them what I want them to see," he corrected, his voice hardening slightly. His fingers brushed the tablet's screen with an almost loving touch. "Amazing what subtle edits can do to a narrative. A trim here, a cut there... suddenly self-defense becomes something much darker. And once it's out there, who's going to believe her denials?"

He stood, brushing invisible dust from his designer jeans. The gesture seemed calculated, like everything else about him. "Twenty-four hours, Mr. Butterfield. I suggest you start with her parents – they seemed very protective earlier. I'm sure they'll want to help their daughter avoid any... unpleasantness."

I watched him walk away, his footsteps crunching in the snow with measured precision. Even his exit seemed choreographed, as if he'd practiced it in front of a mirror. The leather messenger bag swung gently at his side, carrying its incriminating digital cargo.

"Well," Ginger said once Thomas was out of earshot, settling more comfortably on the bench beside me, "that was certainly dramatic. Though I notice our friend's flair for theatrical revelations somewhat undermined his negotiating position. Rather like bringing a script to a poker game."

"He's been planning this for a while," I said, still staring at the place where Thomas had vanished. "Probably started working on it the moment he heard about Liam's environmental activism and the conflicts it was causing. Perfect opportunity for someone like him."

"Yes, his timing was remarkably convenient," Ginger agreed, starting to groom a front paw with focused dedication. "Arriving at the B&B just in time to document everything, positioning himself to observe all the key players."

I stood, brushing snow from my coat. "The question is: what's his endgame? Fifty thousand is a lot of money, but for someone wearing a watch that expensive..."

"Perhaps our fashionable friend has debts to match his taste in accessories," Ginger suggested. "Or maybe this is just a trial run – perfect his technique in a small town before moving on to bigger targets." He paused his grooming to fix me with a serious look. "Though I notice his assumption that showing us the truth would somehow make us more compliant suggests a rather fundamental misunderstanding of your particular brand of stubbornness."

"You mean my dedication to justice?"

"I mean your complete inability to leave well enough alone. Rather like your relationship with that smartphone." His whiskers twitched with amusement. "Though in this case, it might actually work in our favor. Our amateur blackmailer seems to have overlooked the fact that giving us proof of Alice's innocence somewhat undermines his negotiating position."

We started walking home, our footsteps crunching in the fresh snow. The night had grown colder, but somehow the weight of what we'd learned made the temperature seem less important.

"So," Ginger said after we'd gone a block in thoughtful silence, "what's our next move? Besides getting me somewhere warm before my whiskers freeze completely."

"First thing tomorrow, we talk to Alice. Get her side of the story properly." I paused under a streetlight, watching the snowflakes dance in its glow. "Find out what they were arguing about, what led to them being on that boat in the first place. Then we figure out how to deal with our friend Thomas without letting him hurt anyone else."

"Assuming he doesn't decide to change the rules," Ginger pointed out, shaking a clump of snow from his left paw. "He strikes me as the type who's used to controlling the narrative. Rather like Emma with her crystal arrangements – absolutely convinced of their own expertise until reality proves otherwise."

"Her parents must have known," I said, pieces clicking into place as we passed the darkened storefronts of Main Street. "That's why they were so protective when we came asking questions. She probably told them everything right after it happened."

"Indeed," Ginger agreed, his tail swishing thoughtfully through the gathering frost. "Though their protective instincts seem considerably more admirable now that we know what they were protecting. Unlike our journalist friend's protection racket."

We walked the rest of the way in contemplative silence, each lost in our own thoughts about justice, truth, and the weight of secrets in small towns. The night wrapped around us like a familiar blanket, while the distant sound of waves reminded us that some truths, like the tide itself, couldn't be held back forever. They could only be channeled, guided, hoped to flow in the right direction.

The porch light welcomed us home, its warm glow pushing back the winter darkness. Tomorrow would bring what it brought – confrontations and confessions, truths finally spoken aloud. But for now, we had knowledge on our side, even if it wasn't quite the knowledge we'd expected to find.

As I unlocked the door, letting us into the warmth of home, I couldn't help but think about Alice – alone in her room, carrying the weight of that tragic night. Tomorrow, we'd help her share that burden. Tomorrow, we'd find a way to turn this story toward justice rather than profit.

# Chapter 17

The morning sun had barely cleared the horizon when Ginger and I set out for Alice's house again, our path marked by fresh footprints in the snow that had continued falling through the night. The winter air carried that particular crispness that makes breathing feel like sipping ice water.

"I don't suppose we could have waited for a more civilized hour," Ginger commented, delicately picking his way through the snow. "Though I realize our twenty-four-hour deadline does somewhat limit our scheduling options."

"Better use that time while we have it," I replied quietly.

We'd barely touched our breakfast – me managing half a piece of toast while Ginger conducted what he called a "tactical sampling" of his morning tuna. The revelations from last night's meeting with Thomas felt too urgent to waste time on proper meals. Each step through the fresh snow carried the weight of responsibility – knowing the truth but also knowing how easily that truth could be twisted.

Alice's house looked different in the morning light – less imposing than during our previous visit, though no less well-maintained. Smoke curled from the chimney in precise spirals, suggesting someone was already up and about. Through a kitchen window, I caught glimpses of movement – the familiar morning choreography of a family starting their day.

"At least someone's having a proper breakfast," Ginger observed as we approached the porch, his nose twitching at the scent of bacon drifting through the cold air.

The porch steps creaked under my weight – solid oak protesting the cold as much as the intrusion. I knocked on the door, the sound seeming unnaturally loud in the morning quiet. After a moment, it opened, revealing Alice's father in what appeared to be his work clothes – heavy canvas pants and a thick flannel shirt, with steel-toed boots already laced. His expression hardened when he recognized me.

He started to close the door, the movement carrying the weight of parental protection rather than rudeness, but I spoke quickly: "Wait. I know what happened. I know about the accident with Liam."

His hand stilled on the door, fingers tightening on the frame. "What did you say?"

"I know the truth," I kept my voice low, aware of potential neighbors despite the early hour. "About Alice defending herself. About Liam falling. I want to help."

He studied me for a long moment, his face showing the careful calculation of a father weighing risks against possibilities. Finally, he checked his watch – a practical, well-worn timepiece that spoke of years of reliable service. "Got twenty minutes before I need to head to work." He stepped back, opening the door wider. "Better make it quick."

The house's interior carried the competing aromas of coffee, bacon, and whatever floral air freshener someone had recently sprayed. Family photos lined the hallway – many of them featured boats or water, the progression of Alice from toddler to teenager always seeming to include the harbor as a backdrop.

The kitchen radiated warmth from both the stove and the people gathered around it. Alice's mother stood at the counter, spatula in hand, orchestrating what appeared to be her husband's breakfast. Her floral apron had seen better days but remained meticulously clean, much like everything else in the kitchen. Alice sat at the table, a half-eaten piece of toast in front of her suggesting appetite had become optional lately.

She looked up as we entered, her face showing that particular pallor of someone who'd been having conversations with their ceiling all night instead of sleeping. She wore what appeared to be her bakery uniform – crisp white shirt and black pants – though her usual precise appearance seemed slightly rumpled.

"Mr. Butterfield knows about the accident," her father announced without preamble, his voice carrying the particular tone of someone ripping off a bandage. "Says he wants to help."

Alice's mother's spatula clattered against the stovetop, while Alice herself seemed to shrink slightly in her chair. The morning light streaming through the kitchen window caught the fear in both their faces – a fear that had probably become a constant companion these past few days.

"Please, sit," Alice's mother gestured toward an empty chair, her hands showing only the slightest tremor. "Have you had breakfast? I could-"

"Already eaten, thank you," I said, settling into the offered seat. The chair was solid oak, worn smooth by years of family meals. Ginger had already claimed the windowsill, positioning himself to catch both the morning sun and an optimal view of the proceedings.

I went straight to the point, keeping my voice steady despite the gravity of what I had to share. The kitchen seemed to grow smaller as I explained about Thomas, about his video and his blackmail attempt. With each detail, the atmosphere grew heavier, like the air before a storm.

Alice's father's reaction was immediate and explosive. He shot up from his chair, sending it scraping across the linoleum with a sound that made everyone wince. "Where is he?" His voice carried the kind of fury that suggested Thomas's expensive glasses were about to become significantly less intact. "That B&B, right? I'll go have a word with him right now."

"A 'word' that would probably result in assault charges," Ginger observed dryly. "Though I must admit, watching our fashionable friend try to maintain his dignity while running from an angry father does have a certain appeal."

"We'll deal with him," I said quickly, holding up a placating hand. "Together. But first, I need to hear everything. Alice's side of the story. The whole truth."

Alice's hands twisted in her lap, her fingers working against each other like she was trying to untangle invisible knots. The morning light caught the shadows under her eyes, making them look like bruises. "I don't... it's hard to talk about."

"I know," I said gently. "But the more I understand, the better I can help protect you from Thomas. He's trying to twist the truth – we need to know exactly what that truth is."

She glanced at her parents, receiving small nods of encouragement. Her mother had abandoned any pretense of cooking, the bacon now developing a rather dramatic char on the stove. The kitchen filled with the scent of burning breakfast, but no one seemed to notice or care.

"It started so differently," Alice began, her voice barely above a whisper. "When I first met Liam, he was... he was wonderful. Patient, kind, so passionate about marine life. He'd take me out on his rental boats, teach me about different species, show me how to read the water." A small smile touched her lips, though it carried more sadness than joy. "We'd spend hours just drifting, watching seabirds, talking about everything and nothing."

Her expression hardened slightly, like watching a sunny day cloud over. "But lately things changed. After that Christmas party at the Salty Breeze – it was like something snapped in him. His environmental activism became... aggressive. Confrontational. He started drinking more, picking fights with the fishermen. Everything became about his cause, about exposing what he saw as wrongdoing."

"The transformation of passionate advocate to zealot," Ginger commented quietly from his perch.

Alice's hands had stilled in her lap, but the tension radiated from her shoulders like heat from the neglected stove. "We started arguing more. About his approach, about the drinking, about everything really. He never... he never hit me or anything. Not until that last night. But he'd get so angry, so intense. It was like watching someone I cared about disappear into someone I didn't recognize anymore."

Her mother had finally noticed the burning bacon, quickly moving the pan off the heat. The acrid smell lingered in the air, mixing with the growing weight of confession.

"That evening, I'd talked to my parents," Alice continued, glancing at her mother who had begun stress-cleaning the stovetop with rather aggressive enthusiasm. "I'd already decided I wanted to end things with Liam, but I needed... I don't know, permission maybe? Confirmation that I wasn't giving up too easily?"

Her father had resumed his seat, though his posture suggested he was still considering a visit to the B&B. "We told her she was making the right choice," he said gruffly. "That boy was heading down a dark path. Not because of what he believed in – protecting the ocean is a fine cause. But his methods, his anger... that wasn't going to end well."

Alice nodded, absently straightening her bakery uniform's collar. "So I called him that night, asked to meet. That was my mistake – I should have waited, done it somewhere public maybe. But I wanted it over with." She swallowed hard, her hands resuming their nervous movement. "He told me to come to his rental shack. When I got there... he was drunker than he'd sounded on the phone, agitated about something."

The morning light filled the kitchen completely now, illuminating dust motes that danced in the air like tiny stars. Through the window, I could see neighbors beginning their day – cars backing out of driveways, people heading to work, the normal rhythm of life continuing despite the weight of secrets being shared in this warm kitchen.

"He told me someone had broken in while he was napping after my call," Alice continued, her voice growing quieter. "Said it was dark, but he was sure it was one of the fishermen. He'd tried to punch them but hit the wall instead. His knuckles were all bloody…" She trailed off, lost in the memory.

Her mother had abandoned the stove cleaning, now leaning against the counter as if needing its support. "You never told us about the break-in," she said softly.

Alice shrugged, a small movement that seemed to carry the weight of recent history. "It didn't seem important, after… after everything else. But he was so angry about it, kept drinking while telling me about it. When I tried to suggest maybe we should talk another time, he insisted we go out on his boat. Said being on the water would calm him down."

"I argued against it," she added quickly, as if expecting judgment. "Told him he was in no state to be operating a boat. But he said if I didn't go with him, he'd just drink more, maybe take the boat out alone. I thought… I thought maybe I could talk some sense into him once we were out there."

"The water was calm that night," Alice continued, her gaze distant as if watching the scene replay through the kitchen window. "Too calm maybe, like it was holding its breath. We just drifted along the docks while Liam ranted about the fishermen, about how he was going to expose all of them, make them pay for what they were doing to 'his' ocean."

Her hands had begun twisting in her lap again, the morning light catching a small scar on her right palm –

probably from years of kitchen work. "When we got near Mr. Reeve's boat, I tried to reason with him. Told him his aggressive approach was pushing people away, making them defensive instead of willing to listen. That's when he..." She swallowed hard, her voice catching. "That's when he completely lost control."

"The first swing caught me off guard," she admitted, unconsciously touching her shoulder where Liam's hand had probably grabbed her. "I'd never seen him like that before – it wasn't just anger anymore, it was like something had broken inside him. I managed to dodge, scratch him a bit in defense. He kept coming at me, lunging and grabbing. Each time I barely managed to slip away, using the boat's movement to keep my balance while he stumbled after me."

The kitchen had grown unnaturally quiet, even the usual morning sounds of the neighborhood seeming muted, as if giving space to this difficult retelling.

"When he tried to push me overboard..." Alice's voice cracked slightly. "I just reacted, stepped aside. But he was so drunk, so uncoordinated... his own momentum carried him right over the side. The sound when he hit Mr. Reeve's boat was so sharp and sudden...." She pressed her hands against her ears as if trying to block out the memory.

"I screamed for help," Alice continued, dropping her hands back to her lap. "Kept watching the water, waiting for him to surface. But there was nothing – just these little ripples spreading out, like... like water was just swallowing him up. I knew calling an ambulance would be pointless – they'd never get there in time. And jumping in after him..." She shuddered. "In that cold water, in the dark? I'd have just become another victim."

Her mother had moved to stand behind her chair, placing her hands on Alice's shoulders in a gesture of support that seemed automatic, ingrained by years of comforting her daughter through smaller crises.

"So I docked the boat," Alice said, her voice stronger now, as if getting past the worst part had somehow steadied her. "All those hours practicing with Dad and Liam finally paid off, I guess. Then I ran home and told my parents everything. They said... they said not to tell anyone. That the police would just blame me, like they tried to blame you, Mr. Butterfield, when Peter Johnson died."

I nodded, remembering all too well how quickly Miller had jumped to conclusions in that case. "They weren't wrong," I admitted. "Miller's already written this off as an accident or suicide – actually investigating would mean more paperwork than he's willing to deal with."

"The next morning, when I heard the sirens..." Alice's hands had finally stilled, though tension still radiated from her shoulders despite her mother's comforting presence. "For a moment, I thought maybe they'd found him alive somehow. But when I got to the docks and saw his body in those nets... I just couldn't stay there. I called Sophie, asked for some time off, and came straight home."

"That explains her rather hasty departure that morning," Ginger observed, pausing in his morning grooming to watch Alice with unexpected sympathy.

"That story matches perfectly with what's on Thomas's video," I said, leaning forward slightly. "It shows exactly what you've described – self-defense, an accident. But Thomas thinks he can edit it to tell a different story."

Alice's father's hands clenched into fists on the table. "Then we make him delete it. Now. Before he has the chance."

"Look," I said carefully, watching their faces. "I understand wanting to confront Thomas directly. But he's not an amateur at this – he probably has multiple copies of that video stored somewhere safe. If we handle this wrong, he could release it just out of spite."

"Then what do you suggest?" Alice's mother asked, her hands still resting protectively on her daughter's shoulders. "We can't let him blackmail us forever."

I stood, my chair scraping softly against the linoleum. The morning light had strengthened further, turning the kitchen into a stage for what felt like a pivotal moment in this ongoing drama. "First, we talk to him. All of us together. Show him we're united, that we know the truth. Maybe we can reason with him, make him understand that his edited version won't hold up under scrutiny."

"And if that doesn't work?" Alice's father asked, though he seemed less inclined toward immediate violence now.

"Then we deal with that when it comes," I said, trying to project more confidence than I felt. "But right now, Thomas is expecting me to come back alone, acting as his intermediary. Seeing all of us together might throw him off balance enough to make a mistake."

"The element of surprise," Ginger observed, stretching languidly before jumping down from his windowsill.

"I'll call work then, tell them I'm taking a personal day," Alice's father said, already reaching for his phone. "We'll go talk to this journalist together."

The morning had fully arrived now, the sun climbing higher in a sky that promised more snow later. In his room at the B&B, Thomas was probably congratulating himself on his clever scheme, unaware that his carefully constructed plan was about to face something he hadn't counted on – the truth, backed by the kind of solidarity that only small towns can produce when one of their own is threatened.

# Chapter 18

The January morning had grown colder as we stepped out of Alice's house, our breath forming small clouds in the frigid air. Frank Wilson – Alice's father had finally introduced himself properly – was already at his car, scraping frost from the windshield with methodical precision.

His wife Eleanor stood in the doorway, wrapping her cardigan tighter against the cold while watching her husband work. The morning light caught the worry lines around her eyes, making them seem deeper than before. Alice hovered uncertainly behind her mother, her bakery uniform looking oddly formal amid the morning's tension.

"Just need to warm her up a bit," Frank called over his shoulder, his breath visible in the cold air. "Engine gets temperamental in this weather." The car – a well-maintained but aging Volvo station wagon – coughed to life with a sound that suggested it shared its owner's reluctance for early morning adventures.

"Mr. Wilson appears to approach car maintenance with the same intensity he applies to potential violence against blackmailers," Ginger observed, watching Frank attack a particularly stubborn patch of frost. "Though I must say, his windshield scraping technique shows remarkable attention to detail."

As the car's engine warmed with a series of grumbling protests, Ginger suddenly pressed against my leg. "A word, if you please," he meowed quietly. "Somewhere private."

I followed him around the corner of the house, out of earshot from the others. The morning sun had begun to melt some of the fresh snow, creating tiny droplets that caught the light like scattered diamonds. A cardinal watched us from a nearby bush, its bright plumage adding a splash of color to the winter morning.

"Remember last night at the docks?" Ginger began, settling into what I recognized as his 'I know something you don't know' pose. "When you were fumbling with your phone trying to check the time?"

"I wasn't fumbling," I protested automatically. "I was just..."

"Yes, yes, conducting an advanced study in technological incompetence," he waved a paw dismissively. "The point is, you accidentally activated the voice recorder. And it kept running."

I stared at him. "What?"

"All night," he confirmed, his whiskers twitching with barely contained amusement. "Through the entire meeting with our fashionable friend, the walk home, everything until you fell asleep. I noticed the red recording light on the front of the camera when you started snoring – rather impressively, I might add. Had to turn it off myself. Thank goodness you haven't figured out how to password protect that technological menace. Two taps was all it took – unlock screen, stop recording."

The implications hit me like a physical blow. "You mean we have…"

"A recording of Thomas's entire blackmail attempt? Yes." Ginger's tail swished with satisfaction. "Though I should mention I haven't actually listened to it. The quality might be questionable, given your pocket's tendency to muffle everything except those meditation apps Emma keeps installing."

"Why didn't you tell me sooner?"

"Wanted to hear Alice's version first," he replied, starting to groom a front paw with careful precision. "Make sure the stories matched. Besides, watching you fumble through this morning's confrontation had its own entertainment value."

The cardinal had moved closer, apparently deciding we weren't a threat to its morning routine. It hopped through the snow, leaving tiny tracks that reminded me of the evidence we'd been gathering – small marks that together formed a larger picture.

"We need to get Thomas to the police station," I said slowly, the beginnings of a plan forming. "Get him to incriminate himself in front of Miller."

"Ah yes, our esteemed sheriff has such an impressive track record with evidence," Ginger commented dryly. "Though I suppose even he couldn't ignore an actual recording of attempted blackmail. Assuming, of course, your pocket didn't transform it into an unintelligible symphony of fabric sounds."

The sound of the car's engine had settled into a steady idle, suggesting Frank had deemed it sufficiently warmed. His voice carried around the corner: "Jim? You about ready?"

"Coming," I called back, then turned to Ginger. "Let's just hope Thomas takes the bait."

"Indeed," Ginger agreed, rising and shaking snow from his paws. "Though given his apparent fondness for dramatic revelations, I suspect subtlety won't be necessary. Rather like your relationship with modern technology."

We returned to find the Wilsons already settling into the car, Frank behind the wheel while Eleanor fussed over Alice in the back seat. I opened the passenger door and slid into the front seat, Ginger settling onto my lap with his usual precise dignity. The car pulled away from the curb, heading toward the B&B through streets still covered in fresh snow. The car's heater worked overtime against the winter chill, creating a background hum that filled the initial silence.

"If you don't mind me asking," I said carefully, "what kind of work do you both do?"

Frank's hands adjusted on the steering wheel. "Construction, mostly. Different sites around the county, wherever they need an extra pair of hands." He glanced in the rearview mirror at his wife. "Eleanor works part-time at the medical center."

"Which means," he added, his voice tightening slightly, "we definitely don't have fifty thousand dollars to give away."

Alice sat perfectly still in the back seat, her hands folded in her lap with the kind of precision that spoke of barely contained anxiety.

The B&B loomed ahead, its Victorian architecture somehow more imposing in the morning light. The building that had once hosted Lily Robinson's treasure hunt adventures now seemed to hold darker secrets. Fresh snow covered the front steps, unmarked except for a single set of footprints that suggested Thomas had recently stepped out.

As if summoned by our arrival, the front door opened. Thomas emerged, his expensive wool coat a sharp contrast to Frank's practical work clothes. His designer glasses caught the morning light, momentarily transforming the lenses into mirrors that reflected our approach.

His carefully maintained composure cracked slightly when he saw all of us emerging from the car. The messenger bag containing his tablet was clutched protectively against his side, his manicured fingers white-knuckled on the leather strap.

"What is this?" he demanded, his voice carrying more anger than professional detachment now. "I told you to come alone."

"Change of plans," I said mildly, noting how his free hand kept checking his coat pocket – probably making sure a backup copy of the video was secure.

Frank stepped forward, his work boots crunching in the snow with ominous purpose. "We need to talk about that video you're so proud of."

Thomas retreated a step, his expensive shoes leaving precise impressions in the fresh snow. "This isn't how this works," he snapped, his cultivated accent slipping slightly to reveal something harder beneath. "There are protocols, procedures..."

"For blackmail?" Frank's voice carried the kind of quiet danger that made Thomas take another step back. "Funny, I didn't realize that was a regulated industry."

"You're making a mistake," Thomas said, his composure cracking further. The morning light caught a bead of sweat on his temple despite the cold. "I was willing to be reasonable, to handle this discreetly. But now?" His laugh carried no humor. "Now the price has doubled."

Eleanor gasped softly, her hand finding Alice's shoulder in an automatic gesture of protection. Alice herself remained silent, though her face had gone pale at Thomas's words.

"Double?" Thomas continued, warming to his theme now that he thought he had the upper hand. "Yes, I think that's fair compensation for this level of unprofessionalism. One hundred thousand dollars, cash, by tomorrow night. Or..." He patted his coat pocket meaningfully.

"Or what?" I asked, keeping my voice level. "You'll release the video showing exactly what happened? Show everyone how it was self-defense?" I shook my head. "I doubt even your edited version would change anyone's mind about what really happened that night."

Thomas's smile reminded me of documentaries I'd seen about sharks – all teeth and no warmth. "Oh, I've been doing my research on your charming little town. Particularly your law enforcement. Did you know Sheriff Miller has one of the highest conviction rates in the county?" His eyes fixed on Alice with predatory focus. "Mostly because he likes simple solutions. Quick closures. Rather like he tried to pin Peter Johnson's murder on you, Mr. Butterfield."

Alice's face went from pale to absolutely white. Her mother's grip on her shoulder tightened visibly.

"I haven't had time to edit the footage yet," Thomas continued, clearly enjoying the effect his words were having. "But I don't think I'll need to. The original version should be enough to start a police investigation. After all, it clearly shows a confrontation followed by a death."

"The investigation would ruin her life," Eleanor protested, her voice catching. "Even if they eventually found her innocent..."

"Exactly," Thomas's smile widened. "Which is why I'm offering you an alternative. A hundred thousand dollars is a small price to pay for peace of mind, wouldn't you say?"

Frank surged forward, his hands clenched into fists, but I caught his arm. "Wait," I said firmly. "Let's do this properly." I turned to Thomas, whose smile had faltered slightly at Frank's movement. "You want to involve the police? Fine. Let's go to the station right now."

"What?" The word came from several voices at once. Even Ginger looked up at me with surprise, though his expression quickly shifted to understanding.

"Yes," I continued, watching Thomas carefully. "Let's show Miller your video. Let him see exactly what happened that night."

Thomas's composure slipped further, uncertainty creeping into his expression. "That's... that's not how this works," he repeated, but his voice had lost its confident edge.

"I think it is," I countered. "Unless you're worried about something? Something that might come out during an official investigation?"

The implications hung in the morning air like frost. Thomas's eyes darted between us, calculations clearly running behind his designer glasses.

"Fine," he said finally, his jaw tight. "Let's involve the police. I'm sure Sheriff Miller will be very interested in what I have to show him." His eyes narrowed behind those expensive glasses. "Though I should warn you – you'll regret not taking the simpler option. All of you."

"Our pompous friend seems remarkably eager to walk into his own trap," Ginger observed as we headed back to Frank's car.

"Almost too eager," I murmured, watching Thomas climb into his rental car – another expensive choice that seemed designed to impress.

"Indeed," Ginger agreed, settling onto my lap. "Though I notice his confidence might be somewhat misplaced, given the recording currently residing in your pocket. Assuming, of course, your technological ineptitude has accidentally created useful evidence rather than an avant-garde sound installation."

As we pulled away from the B&B, following Thomas's sleek rental toward the police station, Frank glanced at me from behind the wheel.

"Why?" he asked, his voice carrying poorly concealed anxiety. "Why agree to the police so quickly? It will only complicate things, start an official investigation."

I smiled slightly. "There won't be any additional investigation. I know Miller better than Thomas does." I met his questioning gaze as he navigated a turn. "After I came to town and solved several cases – including my own when Miller suspected me – he won't risk making the same mistake twice and try to blame Alice for something she didn't do. He knows I'll get to the truth." I patted my pocket meaningfully. "Besides, I've got a little trick up my sleeve. Or rather, in my pocket."

The clouds had thickened overhead, promising more snow soon. The police station stood ahead, its brick facade stern and official in the winter morning. Thomas's car pulled into the parking lot with the kind of precision that suggested he was still completely confident in his plan.

He had no idea what was waiting in my pocket – an accidental recording that might just turn his carefully constructed scheme into something entirely different than what he'd planned.

# Chapter 19

The police station's reception area smelled of stale coffee and fresh donuts, a combination that seemed uniquely law enforcement. The worn linoleum floor bore scuff marks from generations of boots, while outdated wanted posters curled slightly at the corners of the bulletin board. A dusty ficus plant drooped in one corner, clearly wondering how it had ended up in law enforcement.

Miller sat behind his desk, powdered sugar dusting his uniform like fresh snow, a half-eaten chocolate glazed donut positioned carefully on a napkin beside a stack of untouched paperwork. His coffee mug bore the faded inscription "World's Okayest Sheriff" – a gift from his officers that seemed more accurate than amusing.

The fluorescent lights cast an unflattering glow over everything, making Thomas's expensive clothes look suddenly garish rather than sophisticated. His designer glasses caught the harsh light as he strode forward, tablet already in hand, radiating the particular confidence of someone who thinks they're about to win.

"Sheriff Miller," Thomas announced, his voice carrying that practiced authority that probably worked better in city boardrooms than small-town police stations. "I have evidence regarding Liam Taylor's death that you need to see immediately."

Miller looked up from his donut with the enthusiasm of someone being asked to do actual police work before noon. A small avalanche of powdered sugar drifted onto his desk calendar – which still showed January 1st – as he sighed. "Evidence, huh?"

"Indeed," Thomas smiled, looking around at his captive audience. "Something that will change everything about this case."

"Does he rehearse these dramatic pronouncements in front of a mirror?" Ginger wondered aloud, though of course only I could hear him. "His delivery suggests hours of practice with his reflection."

Thomas was already pulling up the video, his manicured fingers moving across the screen with fluid precision. "Here," he said, positioning the tablet with theatrical precision. "Watch carefully."

The familiar scene played out on the screen – Liam's rental boat approaching the docks, the confrontation, the tragic fall. Miller watched with the kind of detached interest he usually reserved for parking violations, occasionally reaching for his donut without taking his eyes off the screen. A young officer peeked around the door frame, drawn by the sound of the video, only to quickly retreat when Miller glanced his way.

When the video ended, Thomas stood expectantly, practically vibrating with anticipation. His smile showed too many teeth, like a game show host waiting to reveal the grand prize. His Italian leather shoes squeaked slightly on the linoleum as he shifted his weight.

"Well?" he prompted when Miller remained silent. "Clearly this requires immediate action. An arrest warrant perhaps?"

Miller brushed powdered sugar from his mustache, considering. The clock on the wall ticked loudly in the silence, its hands suggesting it was time to replace the battery. "Nope," he said finally. "Pretty clear accident case to me. Drunk guy gets aggressive, falls in. Happens more often than you'd think around here."

The relief that swept through the Wilson family was almost palpable. Frank's shoulders dropped from their defensive posture, while Eleanor's death grip on her daughter's arm relaxed slightly. Color began returning to Alice's face, replacing the ghostly pallor she'd worn since entering the station.

"But... but..." Thomas sputtered, his carefully maintained composure cracking like thin ice. "Did you not see the confrontation? The struggle? She practically pushed him!"

"Not what I saw," Miller shrugged, reaching for his coffee. The mug left a ring on his desk calendar, adding to an impressive collection. "Saw self-defense. Girl trying to keep her distance from a drunk man on a boat. Physics did the rest." He took a long sip, then added almost accusingly, "Why didn't you bring this in sooner? Could've closed this case days ago, saved me a lot of paperwork."

"Our esteemed sheriff's dedication to avoiding effort continues to impress," Ginger observed dryly. "Though I notice his ability to recognize self-defense improves remarkably when it means less forms to fill out."

I fought back a smile, recognizing the fundamental flaw in Thomas's plan. He'd done his research on Miller's conviction rates but missed the most important fact about our local sheriff – his profound dedication to avoiding unnecessary work. Given a choice between a complex investigation and a simple accident ruling, Miller would choose the path of least resistance every time.

"This is outrageous!" Thomas's voice had risen several octaves, his accent slipping further. His designer frames slipped down his nose, requiring an agitated adjustment. "I'll release this online! Let the public decide! Social media will-"

"That evidence," Miller interrupted, setting down his coffee with unusual firmness, "is now part of an official police investigation." His voice carried an edge that suggested he was actually going to have to do some work and wasn't happy about it. "Releasing it would be obstruction of justice. You really want to add that to your morning?"

"Speaking of justice," I said carefully, reaching into my pocket where my phone resided. "There's something else you should hear, Sheriff."

Miller's mustache twitched with resignation. "More evidence? Don't suppose this could wait until after lunch?"

"It's important," I assured him, fumbling slightly with my phone. Emma's latest app updates had rearranged all the icons again, turning simple tasks into technological treasure hunts. The screen seemed unnecessarily bright in the fluorescent lighting.

"Perhaps we should alert the Nobel committee about your breakthrough in human-technology relations," Ginger commented dryly from his position near my feet, his tail curling elegantly around his paws. "Though I notice your ability to accidentally activate features continues to be your most reliable skill."

After several attempts that somehow activated what sounded like a tropical rainforest meditation and Emma's cosmic alignment tracker, I finally found the voice recording. A meditation app chimed helpfully in the background, suggesting I align my chakras. "Just... give me a moment," I muttered, feeling my face heat up as multiple pairs of eyes watched my technological struggles.

The recording started with what was unmistakably my voice having a one-sided conversation, punctuated by Ginger's distinct meows and occasional purrs. My face grew warmer as I fumbled to fast-forward through that part.

"Do you... often talk to yourself, Butterfield?" Miller asked, amusement creeping into his tone. A few nearby officers had stopped pretending to work, openly watching the scene unfold.

"It helps me think," I said quickly, finally finding the relevant section. Thomas's voice filled the room, his blackmail demands crisp and clear despite my pocket's attempt to muffle them. The recording captured everything – the threats, the deadline, the amount demanded. Even the sound of waves lapping against the dock came through clearly.

Miller's expression had shifted from amused to serious, his forgotten donut leaving a powdered sugar ring on his desk. The young officer who'd been peeking in earlier was now taking notes, his pen moving frantically across his pad. As the recording played on, Thomas's face went from red to white to an interesting shade of gray that clashed with his designer outfit.

"That's... that's been edited," Thomas protested weakly when the recording finished, his manicured hand clutching his messenger bag like a shield. "Manufactured evidence! You can't possibly-"

"Created in the approximately twelve hours since our meeting?" I asked mildly. "That's quite a technological feat. Especially given my well-documented struggles with basic phone functions. Would you like to watch me try to change my ringtone as proof?"

"Take him to holding," Miller ordered, gesturing to two officers who had been trying very hard to look busy while eavesdropping. His coffee mug scraped across the desk as he reached for a fresh incident report form. "Attempted blackmail, withholding evidence... we'll start with those and see what else turns up."

"You can't do this!" Thomas protested as the officers approached. "Do you know who I am? I have lawyers-"

"Who probably won't be thrilled about explaining blackmail charges to a judge," one of the officers commented, already reaching for his handcuffs.

As the officers led a protesting Thomas away, his expensive shoes squeaking indignantly on the linoleum, I turned to Miller. "You might want to look into his background. Given his expensive tastes and comfort with blackmail, this probably wasn't his first attempt."

"Great," Miller sighed, already reaching for a form with the resigned air of someone facing unavoidable paperwork. His pen squeaked against the paper as he began writing. "More work. Just what I needed today." He looked up at Alice, who had been standing so still she might have been part of the station's sparse decor. "Miss Wilson, I'll need your statement about what happened that night. Shouldn't take long – just need to make everything official."

"We're staying with her," Frank said firmly, his hand finding his daughter's shoulder.

Miller just nodded, probably recognizing that arguing would mean more work. As the Wilsons followed him to an interview room, I settled into one of the hard plastic chairs in the waiting area, Ginger arranging himself comfortably beside me. The chair creaked ominously under my weight, suggesting it had seen better decades.

"Well," he observed, beginning to groom a front paw with focused dedication, "that went more smoothly than expected. Though I notice our fashionable friend's descent from confident blackmailer to arrested suspect lacked a certain theatrical flourish. Rather disappointing, really. Not even one dramatic soliloquy about revenge."

\*\*\*

The station's morning routine continued around us – phones ringing with their unique law enforcement urgency, officers shuffling papers with varying degrees of enthusiasm, the coffee maker in the break room protesting its constant use with alarming sounds. Through the window, I could see more snow beginning to fall, adding another layer to the winter landscape. A parking enforcement officer trudged past, looking about as happy as someone whose job involved making everyone else's day worse.

Dr. Chen appeared from the direction of Miller's office, her practical boots squeaking slightly on the linoleum floor. Her dark hair was pulled back in its usual no-nonsense style. She carried a stack of files that looked significantly more organized than anything on Miller's desk.

"Just saw the video," she said without preamble, settling into the chair across from me. Her files made a soft thump as she set them aside. "I can't believe Miller was actually right about something being an accident. It's like discovering your broken clock finally showed the correct time."

"Life is full of surprises," I agreed, sharing her obvious amusement at Miller's accidental competence. The wall clock ticked steadily behind us as I filled her in on the additional details – Mike Sullivan's break-in, Liam's increasing aggression, the events that led to that final confrontation.

Dr. Chen nodded, her expression thoughtful. The fluorescent light caught her glasses as she leaned forward. "That explains the bruised knuckles – probably from when he hit the wall during the break-in. And the head injury..." She paused, considering her words carefully. "The angle and force are consistent with someone falling and striking the side of a boat. Especially if alcohol had affected their coordination."

"It's rather refreshing to encounter actual scientific analysis," Ginger commented, pausing his grooming to watch Dr. Chen with approval. "Unlike certain law enforcement officials who consider donuts a major food group and gut feelings valid evidence."

The interview room door opened with a soft creak, releasing the Wilsons back into the waiting area. Dr. Chen gathered her files, excusing herself with a quick nod.

"Back to my quiet kingdom," she said, heading toward the morgue. "At least the dead don't argue with my findings."

Miller followed the family out, his attention already focused on his next donut with the single-minded determination he usually reserved for avoiding complex cases. A fresh powdered sugar stain decorated his uniform.

"No problems?" I asked as the Wilsons approached. The relief on their faces was answer enough, but Frank spoke anyway.

"None," he confirmed, some of the tension finally leaving his shoulders. "Miller believed Alice's story completely. The video just confirmed what she told him." He paused, studying me with newfound respect. "How did you know it would work out this way?"

"Even better," Eleanor added, smoothing her cardigan with still-shaking hands. "He seemed annoyed that we'd taken up so much of his morning with something so straightforward."

I smiled slightly, watching Miller settle back behind his desk. "In the past few months, I've learned two things about our sheriff – his love of simple solutions and his hatred of paperwork. A clear accident case means minimal forms to fill out." I patted my pocket where my phone resided. "Though having evidence of attempted blackmail probably helped focus his attention."

"About that recording," Eleanor said, her hands finally still after days of nervous movement. Her wedding ring caught the light as she gestured. "How did you manage to capture the whole conversation?"

"Apparently I accidentally activated the voice recorder last night," I admitted, carefully not mentioning how I'd discovered this fact. "Only noticed it this morning before we headed to the B&B. Sometimes technology works in mysterious ways."

"Your technological incompetence has finally proved useful," Ginger observed. "Perhaps we should alert Emma – she'll want to consult her crystals about this miraculous development."

Alice spoke for the first time since leaving the interview room, her voice carrying equal parts relief and resignation. Her bakery uniform seemed less crisp now, as if the morning's tension had affected even the fabric. "The whole town will know everything soon. Miller's officers aren't exactly known for their discretion."

As if to prove her point, two officers walked past, already whispering about the morning's events. Their conversation died quickly when they noticed us watching, but their hasty retreat said enough.

"We've decided to send Alice to her grandparents for a while," Eleanor added, her hand finding her daughter's arm again. The gesture seemed automatic, maternal. "Just until things settle down. They have a lovely place up the coast – quiet, away from all this."

"This town needs good bakers," I said, watching Alice's face carefully. The morning light through the station windows illuminated the determination in her eyes, despite her obvious exhaustion. "Will you come back?"

She nodded, a small smile touching her lips. "Of course. I just need some time to process everything. And maybe let the initial wave of gossip pass." She glanced at her parents, receiving encouraging nods. "Besides, Sophie's already talking about making me a partner at the bakery when I return. Says my croissants are better than hers."

"High praise indeed," Ginger observed, his whiskers twitching with amusement. "Though I reserve judgment until I've conducted a proper taste test. For investigative purposes only, of course. Quality control is essential in our line of work."

"Thank you," Frank said suddenly, extending his hand. The morning light caught the calluses earned from years of honest work. "For everything. Not just helping Alice, but for understanding. For seeing the truth instead of just assuming the worst."

I shook his hand, feeling the strength of his grip. "Sometimes the truth isn't what we expect. Doesn't make it any less true."

The Wilsons gathered their coats, preparing to face the falling snow outside. The station's front door creaked open as another officer entered, bringing a gust of cold air and the sound of the town starting its day.

Alice paused at the door, looking back with equal parts gratitude and determination in her expression. Her hand rested briefly on the doorframe, like she was memorizing the moment. "I'll be back," she said firmly. "This is my home. I won't let gossip chase me away forever."

As they disappeared into the swirling snow outside, I turned to Ginger. Through the window, I could see their figures growing smaller against the white landscape, heading toward whatever came next.

"Salty Breeze tonight?" I suggested. "I think we've earned a drink."

"Indeed," he agreed, stretching elegantly before hopping down from his perch. "Though I notice our tendency to celebrate case closures at Shawn's establishment suggests a certain predictability in our routine. Not that I'm complaining – his cream selection has improved remarkably since our last investigation."

The snow continued to fall outside, blanketing the town in fresh white silence. Somewhere in a holding cell, Thomas was probably realizing that his carefully constructed scheme had crumbled like a poorly made croissant. And soon, Alice would return to her ovens, proving that even in small towns, second chances could rise like well-kneaded dough.

But for now, we had a warm bar waiting and friends who would want to hear the whole story. Though perhaps I'd leave out the part about accidentally recording evidence through sheer technological incompetence. Some details, after all, were better left between a man and his cat.

# Chapter 20

Heat and conversation washed over us as we pushed through the Salty Breeze's heavy wooden door, leaving winter's bite behind. Chet Baker floated from the ancient jukebox, its sound softened by decades of faithful service. The bar's familiar scents welcomed us – decades of spilled beer soaked into wood, tobacco smoke lingering in the corners despite years of being smoke-free, and something spicy and inviting from Shawn's latest cocktail experiments.

The evening regulars had settled into their places – Robert hunched over his dark beer at the bar's worn edge, while Emma held court amid a carefully arranged collection of crystals that caught the low light. Her outfit tonight outdid even her usual mystical attire – some kind of dress covered in actual twinkling lights arranged in constellations. Behind the bar, Shawn moved with practiced grace, each glass in his hands catching the warm light as he polished it to perfection.

"Finally!" Shawn's welcome carried over the evening murmur as we approached. He was already pulling down my special glass. "Was beginning to think you'd gotten lost in all this paperwork Miller's probably avoiding."

"Nearly did," I admitted, settling onto my familiar barstool. "Though I blame Emma's technological improvements to my phone. That cosmic alignment tracker went off right when I was trying to find the voice recorder icon."

Emma brightened, her numerous bangles creating a symphony of tiny chimes as she turned toward me. "Oh! Did the celestial alignment app help during the crisis? I specially programmed it to harmonize with Venus's current position."

"Is that why it started playing tropical rainforest meditation just when I wanted to play the recording?" I asked dryly. "Something about nature sounds aligning with justice?"

"The stars work in mysterious ways," Emma said serenely, adjusting a particularly large crystal. "Though I should mention that Mercury is still in retrograde, which might explain why your phone kept switching to Spanish."

Ginger, who had claimed his usual spot beside me, eyed the impressive array of cream varieties Shawn had set before him. "I see some new additions to the feline refreshment options," he observed. "Though I notice the presentation suggests someone's been taking lessons from Mrs. Abernathy's culinary standards."

The evening crowd had begun filtering in, their conversations creating a comfortable background hum. Through the windows, snow continued to fall, transforming the street outside into something from a winter postcard. The warm glow of the bar's lights created pools of golden illumination that seemed to hold back the darkness beyond the glass.

"By the way," Robert said, turning his beer mug between calloused hands, "heard some interesting versions of what happened at the station this morning. According to Mrs. Henderson, there was some kind of international spy ring involved."

Shawn chuckled, setting my finished cocktail before me with practiced precision. "That's nothing. Chuck was in here earlier telling everyone it was all about stolen fishing technology. Something about underwater cameras and government secrets."

"The cosmic energies did suggest hidden truths would come to light," Emma added, shifting her crystals around with mystical purpose. "But even my star charts didn't predict the blackmail angle."

"Speaking of predictions," Ginger commented, delicately sampling each cream variety with careful consideration, "I notice our local rumor mill continues to operate with its usual efficiency, if not accuracy. Though I must say, the international spy theory shows remarkable creativity."

The door opened, bringing a gust of cold air and a group of fishermen including Mike Sullivan. His crew found a table in the corner, their usual boisterous behavior somewhat subdued. Mike caught my eye as he passed, offering a slight nod that carried more meaning than casual acknowledgment. I returned the gesture, hoping he'd keep his word about the fishing quotas. Earlier that day, after leaving the police station, I'd called Dylan – the passionate environmental activist from the protest – and shared a carefully edited version of events.

"Just keep an eye on things," I'd suggested during that call. "But remember Liam's mistakes. Passion for a cause is admirable, but aggression and alcohol only cloud the waters."

Dylan had been quiet for a moment, processing everything. "We'll watch," he'd finally agreed. "Not just Sullivan's crew, but all of them. Continue what Liam started – just maybe with better methods."

The jukebox had shifted to something more upbeat – Ray Charles filling the bar with warmth that seemed to match the atmosphere. A fresh wave of customers entered, shaking snow from their coats and stamping boots on the mat by the door. The weekday evening crowd was building, a mix of regulars and people drawn in by the weather and the promise of Shawn's special winter cocktails.

"I still can't believe Miller actually handled something correctly," Robert mused, his voice carrying a hint of grudging admiration. "Though I suppose even a broken clock is right twice a day."

"Funny, Dr. Chen made a similar observation this morning," I said, taking a sip of my perfectly crafted Librarian cocktail. "But actually, I think Miller was more motivated by avoiding paperwork than anything else. A clear accident case means minimal forms to fill out."

"Indeed," Ginger agreed, moving on to sample what appeared to be a new variety of cream Shawn had acquired specially for him. "Though I notice our esteemed sheriff's dedication to simplicity aligns remarkably well with his dedication to donut consumption. Both require minimal effort."

The door chimed again, and to everyone's surprise, Sophie entered. She paused just inside, shaking snow from her sensible winter coat. Unlike her sister Maggie, who had always maintained a carefully crafted image, Sophie looked comfortable in her casual clothes – practical boots, well-worn jeans, and a cable-knit sweater that suggested warmth was more important than appearance.

"Sophie!" Shawn called out, genuine warmth in his voice. "This is unexpected. Can't remember the last time we had a baker grace our humble establishment."

Sophie made her way to our group, settling onto the barstool next to me with none of the affected grace Maggie would have shown. "Maggie avoided places like this," she said, as if reading my thoughts. "Part of her 'perfect baker' persona. But sometimes you need a drink, especially after a week like this one."

Shawn was already crafting something that involved cinnamon and what looked like premium whiskey. He combined the ingredients with the confident flair of a master mixologist at work.

"How's the bakery doing?" Emma asked, her crystals creating gentle chimes as she turned toward Sophie. "I noticed you've been selling out of croissants earlier each day."

Sophie accepted the drink Shawn presented – an amber creation garnished with a twist of orange peel. "Business is good. Though it'll be different without Alice, even if it's just temporary." She took a small sip, eyebrows rising in appreciation. "This is excellent, Shawn. What do you call it?"

"The Baker's Remedy," he grinned, clearly pleased with her reaction. "Seemed appropriate. Don't worry – nothing like those overly sweet concoctions Maggie used to pretend to enjoy at community events."

"I've already found someone to help while Alice is away," Sophie continued, rotating her glass to catch the bar's warm light. "Another of Mrs. Abernathy's former students. That woman has practically trained half the bakers in the county."

"All while maintaining her position as the town's primary source of cookie-based comfort," Ginger observed, having finished his cream tasting with evident satisfaction. "Though I notice her culinary influence extends remarkably well to feline refreshments. Shawn's cream selection has improved significantly since our last visit."

The evening deepened around us, the bar's warmth creating a comfortable bubble against the winter night. Through the windows, snow continued to fall, each flake catching the light before disappearing into the growing drifts. The jukebox had moved on to Ella Fitzgerald, her voice weaving through the conversations like golden thread.

"You know what's ironic?" Robert said suddenly, his face thoughtful in the bar's warm light. "Liam tried to buy my boat last summer. Offered well below market value, said he needed it for his environmental documentation. Now..." He trailed off, the weight of recent events hanging in the air.

"Speaking of money," I said, automatically tracing a ring of condensation on the bar with my finger, "where did Liam even get the funds for all those rental boats? They couldn't have been cheap."

"Actually," Shawn replied, "word is his grandmother left him quite a fortune when she died. Probably hoped he'd use it to start a proper business, not fuel an environmental crusade."

"The stars suggested a complex relationship with inheritance," Emma interjected, her bangles creating gentle music as she gestured. "Though Neptune's influence indicated a strong connection to maritime pursuits."

"Indeed," Ginger commented dryly. "Though I notice celestial interpretations become remarkably more specific after the facts are known. Rather like Miller's investigative skills."

The door opened again, bringing another gust of winter air and a group of locals who'd clearly heard about the morning's events at the police station. Their whispered conversations carried fragments of increasingly elaborate theories about what had really happened. Mrs. Henderson's international spy ring theory had apparently evolved to include underwater bases and secret government experiments.

"People will talk," Sophie said quietly, watching the newcomers find seats. "But Alice is strong. Stronger than most people realize. She'll get through this."

"Sophie," I said, my voice low enough that only our small group could hear, "I need to apologize. I suspected Alice at first, thought she might have..." I trailed off, unable to finish the thought.

Sophie shook her head, a gentle smile touching her lips. "You were just doing your job, Jim. And you weren't entirely wrong about Alice's involvement – even if it turned out to be self-defense and a tragic accident. More importantly, you helped prove that truth."

Emma reached over to pat Sophie's hand, her numerous rings catching the light. "The cards suggest a period of healing followed by renewal. But perhaps that's just common sense rather than mystical insight."

"Speaking of renewal," Sophie said, her expression brightening slightly, "I've been planning something special for Valentine's Day. Only two weeks away, you know. Thought the town could use something to look forward to."

"Oh?" Emma leaned forward, her constellation dress twinkling with the movement. "Do tell! The stars have been hinting at romantic energies in February."

"Nothing too elaborate," Sophie assured us, though her smile suggested otherwise. "Just some special treats, maybe a few themed displays. Mrs. Abernathy's already offered to help with cookies."

"Hopefully this celebration won't involve any mysteries," Ginger remarked, stretching languidly on his perch. "Though given our track record with holidays in this town, perhaps we should prepare for romantic intrigue. Or at least pastry-related peculiarities."

The evening continued to deepen, the bar's warmth creating a comfortable sanctuary against the winter night. Mike and his crew were preparing to leave, their movements carrying the weight of men who knew they were being watched but were determined to prove themselves worthy of second chances. The jukebox had circled back to Chet Baker, his trumpet weaving through the conversations like smoke.

Through the windows, the snow continued its gentle descent, blanketing the town in fresh white. Alice was probably packing for her grandparents' visit in her family's house on Pinewood Street, while Thomas likely stared at the ceiling of his cell, his blackmail scheme now nothing but ashes. But here in the Salty Breeze, surrounded by friends both old and new, the future seemed full of possibilities rather than threats.

"To new beginnings," Shawn proposed, raising his own glass in a toast. "And maybe a few weeks without any murders, mysterious disappearances, or holiday-themed crimes?"

"I wouldn't count on it," Robert chuckled, lifting his beer. "This town seems to attract trouble like a lighthouse attracts ships."

"The stars do suggest some interesting alignments in February," Emma added, her crystals creating a gentle symphony as she raised her glass. "But maybe we should focus on enjoying Sophie's Valentine treats rather than looking for mysteries."

"Indeed," Ginger agreed, his tail curling with contentment. "But even if we do stumble upon a Valentine's mystery, at least we'll have proper refreshments to sustain us during the investigation."

I smiled, raising my own glass to join the toast. The bar's warm light caught the amber liquid, turning it to gold. Outside, the snow continued to fall, each flake carrying its own small secret to add to the growing blanket of white that covered Oceanview Cove. Tomorrow would bring what it would, but for now, we had this moment – friends gathered together, sharing warmth against the winter night, looking forward to whatever adventures awaited us next.

The end of this case might have marked the close of another chapter in our small-town mysteries, but something told me our story was far from over. Valentine's Day was approaching, after all, and if there's one thing I'd learned about Oceanview Cove, it's that every holiday seemed to bring its own unique brand of intrigue.

But that, as they say, was a mystery for another day.

The End
… of the fourth book in the series

# Jim and Ginger's Next Case

Jim and Ginger return in "*Valentine's Poison*" where they take on the case of a mass poisoning on Valentine's Day.

https://mybook.to/ValentinesPoison

# Bonus Content

Get a FREE Jim and Ginger story!

Enjoy "The Curious Case of the Creeping Hedge" – an exclusive short story not available anywhere else!

Subscribe to Arthur Pearce's newsletter today and receive:

- Your free short story
- Updates on new releases
- Special discounts and cover reveals

https://www.arthurpearce.com/newsletter

# Jim and Ginger's First Case

New to the series? Start with *"Murder Next Door"* where Jim and Ginger take on their first case when a friendly neighbor turns up dead.

https://mybook.to/MurderNextDoor

Printed in Great Britain
by Amazon